IN A FERTILE DESERT

**NORTH
LINCOLNSHIRE**
COUNCIL

IN A FERTILE DESERT

Modern Writing from the United Arab Emirates

Selected and translated by
Denys Johnson-Davies

ARABIA BOOKS
LONDON

First published in Great Britain in 2009 by
Arabia Books
70 Cadogan Place
London SW1X 9AH
www.arabia-books.co.uk

This edition published by arrangement with
The American University in Cairo Press
113 Sharia Kasr el Aini, Cairo, Egypt
420 Fifth Avenue, New York, NY 10018
www.aucpress.com

"The Sound of Singing" appeared in Under the Naked Sky: Short
Stories from the Arab World, selected and translated by Denys
Johnson-Davies (Cairo: The American University in Cairo Press, 2000).

Printed in Great Britain by J. H. Haynes & Co. Ltd., Sparkford

ISBN 978-1-906697-13-6

1 2 3 4 5 6 7 8 9 10   14 13 12 11 10 09
Cover design: Arabia Books
Page design: Adam el Sehemy / AUC Press Design Center

Contents

vi   Contents

Acknowledgments

Thanks are due to the following persons in the United Arab Emirates who helped me to find the stories that make up this volume:

Jumaa Abdulla Alqubaisi, the director of the National Library in Abu Dhabi

Ahmed Rashid Thani, writer, Abu Dhabi

Ibrahim Mubarak, writer, Dubai

Hareb al-Dhaheri, writer and Head of the Union of Emirati Writers, Abu Dhabi

Kamel Yousef Hussein of *al-Bayan* newspaper, Dubai

Mohamed al-Mazrouei, writer and artist, Abu Dhabi, who also provided me with information about the individual writers I chose to include.

My special thanks are also due to the Emirati artist from Dubai, Abdul Qader Al Rais, who has kindly allowed us to use his painting as the cover for this volume.

Introduction

In a short period of time the United Arab Emirates (UAE) has emerged from obscurity to be recognized as a country to be reckoned with in various spheres. Literature, however, has not been one of them. When, therefore, I recently decided to compile a volume of short stories from the Emirates in English translation, I was of two minds about being able to find a sufficient number of stories worth translating. In the world outside the Middle East only one writer from the UAE, my friend Muhammad al-Murr, is known; he has specialized in the short story, of which he has put together some fourteen volumes, while two separate translators have selected stories by him for volumes in English. Were there another nineteen writers living in various parts of the UAE who could provide material for a whole volume? As with all the volumes of short stories I have published, I wished to avoid having any one writer represented by more than one story, which would, in my opinion, suggest that someone represented by, say, two stories was a better writer than one represented by a single tale.

So, with the help of friends in various parts of the country, I set about reading the few available volumes of short stories that had been produced since the genre first became known in this part of the Gulf in the last century. Until very recently, budding writers of short stories had no outlets for publishing their work, instead using the Internet to post their writing, where they at least could have the satisfaction of seeing their stories in print and where fellow writers could follow what others were producing. It thus happened that in my search for short stories, I was told of a story entitled "The Old Woman" by a young woman writer that was to be found on the Internet. Having read and enjoyed the story I decided to translate it and use it in this volume. I had hardly finished translating it when another friend rang me up and told me triumphantly of a story that had just appeared in a local magazine. On looking through the magazine, I found that the story was no other than "The Old Woman." This shows how quickly things are moving in this part of the world—and this takes in the field of creative writing.

The modern movement in Arab literature had its beginnings in the 1940s, with writers such as Egypt's Naguib Mahfouz later achieving recognition worldwide. But the UAE, even before the area came out of British protection and the present federation of states was formed in the early 1970s, was not without an interest in creativity with language. I remember, when I went there in 1969 as director of the very basic local broadcasting station, going out one day with a colleague into the desert to record a local poet. The old man we met was blind and lived a harsh existence in a reed hut. At that time, the type of literature practiced was that of Nabati poetry, which was in the local spoken Arabic. The old man surprised me by reeling off at great speed several hundred lines of this poetry, and I was told that he knew by heart not hundreds but thousands of lines of his own and others' Nabati verse. Today this form of literature is still widely practiced and held in high regard in the UAE.

It was only in the 1970s that the new genres of novel and short story, which had first made their way into Arabic literature through such centers as Cairo, were discovered by readers and potential writers in the UAE. Thus, among the stories in the present volume, the earliest was published in 1974 and the latest a matter of a few months ago. Since I started this project, there has been increasing interest in the area for the arts and literature; these include major projects for the translation into Arabic of more of the world's masterpieces. At the same time new outlets are becoming available for the work of the creative writer. There are now magazines in which short stories make their appearance, and a short while ago the National Library in Abu Dhabi produced several volumes of creative writing, including poetry, volumes of short stories, also an accomplished novella. As more writing appears in print, it is to be hoped that the present first-ever selection of UAE stories translated into English will be followed in due time by yet others, and that local writers will become better known in the rest of the Arab world and will increasingly attract the attention of other translators.

A Decision

Ebtisam al-Mualla

I was sitting on the edge of the bed watching my wife in the mirror as she put blue shadow to her eyes. I felt something approaching guilt invade my whole being. Poor Iona!

If only she knew what had led me to invite her to go out with me, if only she knew of the idea that had been blown up by the stories of my mother and the neighbors and by my friends' rebukes until it had culminated in this decision.

A decision I had taken after long nights of thinking and reluctance.

I grew conscious of Iona's voice asking me in her resonant English accent as she went on looking into the mirror, "Hi, what do you think? I'm ready."

I didn't comment. Something made me stay silent, so I got up and made my way with her to the car and off we went. Reaching out her hand to put on the air-conditioning, Iona said, "It's the first time you've invited me out with you on our own and without my asking you, except for our lovely evenings out in Queensbury and Knightsbridge. Do you remember them, Sultan?"

I lit a cigarette and nodded my head in agreement. It was in the days when I had met Iona by chance. I had been trying to return a suit I'd bought from a shop in Knightsbridge because when I had got back to my hotel, I had discovered that I owned one with a similar color. I tried to persuade the salesman to change it for another, but was unable to do so. He was stubborn and kept on arguing with me over petty details. It was only Iona's help that changed things.

She had quietly intervened and solved the problem with Clive, the shop owner, who I later learned was her cousin. From that day on I would meet up with her and we would often go out to lunch together. These meetings ended with our getting married.

I turned to Iona and saw that she had pulled a cigarette from my packet and begun smoking it while looking out at the lake and the golden lights that encircled it.

Oh, what a long time it had been since I'd been to this place! Before I got married I would meet up with Salem, Mohamed, Ali, and several friends near Lake Khalid, where we'd spread out a small carpet—we always had one in Ali's car—with the voice of the singer Abdel Haleem Hafez ringing out from my car stereo, and we'd play cards. We'd drink tea of an evening and listen to Mohamed's amusing anecdotes.

When I had returned with Iona, great changes came about in my life, changes that began in my home. I pleaded long and hard with my mother to let Iona live with us, and when she finally did give her consent I felt that the matter had been settled at the expense of my comfort.

Iona had become, in my mother's view, the beginning of the mistake. When I gave an opinion it would be torn to shreds because my opinions, having led me to marry this blonde foreign girl, were no longer considered sensible. Even when I gave Alya an older brother's advice, my mother would deride it, and all because I had married Iona after Hajj Salem had demanded of me a fortune of several thousands as bridal money for his daughter.

So many difficulties resulted from Iona entering our house! I would yearn for some rest after a tiring day at work, but no sooner did I enter the house than my mother would unfold a catalog of complaints, most of them utterly trivial. "Iona let the neighbor's cat in through the window, breaking the vase that decorated the table." "Your wife couldn't even wash her own jeans; she threw them in the clothes basket so that we could wash them for her." "Iona turned up the volume of the stereo. . . ." Iona went out without asking permission." And so on.

I suffered patiently, trying to take Iona's side whenever I saw in her eyes a silent plea for me to do something.

Iona would refuse all the solutions I put forward. She would take a stand against me, "I can't help your mother in the kitchen—the smell of fish kills me."

"I won't spend the whole of Sunday shut up in the house just because I'm in this country."

"I can't agree to dressing like your sister Alya—those sorts of clothes make it hard for me to move, and I can't give up smoking in a house so full of problems, and . . . ."

Iona interrupted my train of thought as she stroked away the ash from the cigarette she was holding, sending it all over my dishdasha.

"I wrote at length in my last letter to my mother and my brother Mike," she said quietly, "about your country. I told her how I'd enjoyed my time on the shores of Ajman with your sister Alya and your mother. I described the souks of Dubai at night and I told them a lot about Sharjah. You still have to take me to the capital."

Then I saw that she was gazing at the fountain in the middle of the lake.

"Pretty, isn't it?" she asked me. "Don't they sell postage stamps of it?"

I had seen several stamps for sale in Indian kiosks, stamps depicting Lake Khalid at night, but where would I find them now?

"Perhaps we can buy some stamps tomorrow."

She took a small mirror from her handbag, redid her make-up, then asked me, "Where are we going?"

I looked at the lights that from afar draped the house of Hajj Salem. It was the wedding feast of Aisha, whose husband was a rich merchant able to afford the dowry that had stunned me.

I pointed to the house and said to Iona, "We're going to a wedding feast." I was absolutely certain that Aisha did not like this marriage. I had seen it in her eyes, on the last visit Alya and I had paid her. We arrived at Hajj Salem's house to find that the neighboring open square had been turned into a stage bustling with men, women, and children who had come along to watch the display of folk dancing.

I parked the car near the square. The sounds of singing came to me as I opened the car window and saw Iona's face fill with astonishment: she was seeing a wedding ceremony for the first time since arriving in the country. Open-mouthed, she followed the movements of the men as they swayed with their canes. She seemed overwhelmed as she asked me, "What's this, Sultan?"

I had been expecting a question like that from her. Opening the car door, I answered her, "It's a feast—the daughter of the owner of the house is getting married."

"Does everyone celebrate in the same way? Is this dancing part of the celebration?"

"It's a folk company—most families invite folk companies to take part with them at their wedding parties."

"Can anyone dance with them? You, for instance?"

What ideas Iona had!

Taking hold of the string of prayer beads that hung from the car mirror, I answered her, "Perhaps some people could, but not me—I don't know how."

"But they're easy movements. What do they call it?"

"Al-Ayyala."

Iona laughed at the word and tried to pronounce it.

She went on watching the scene. Perhaps she thought I had brought her here for this purpose—to watch a wedding ceremony.

I looked at the wrinkles on Iona's face as she sat alongside me, watching the children in their bright clothes. Her eyes were blue, her face thin and covered with freckles, her lips full. What had I seen in her?

Was what Mohamed had said correct—that I had married Iona to affirm my existence to Hajj Salem?

There were many big differences. Aisha's face, with its propensity for shyness, presented itself before me. Her eyes were black, with hair black as the night; even her voice had an attractive, warm huskiness.

Iona seemed to sense that my mind was busy elsewhere.

"What's wrong, Sultan?"

My fingers played with the prayer beads as I tried to find the words with which to begin my talk with Iona. Should I kill the joy emanating from her eyes?

Trying to sound normal, I said, "Did you know that the bride is an old friend of my sister Alya's and that she often used to visit us?"

With her happy smile still on her lips, Iona asked, "And where's the bride? I'd really like to see her. I'm sure she's very beautiful."

"Yes, she is beautiful and I wanted to marry her."

"Then why didn't you marry her?" Iona asked in astonishment.

"I asked her father."

"And he refused?"

"No, her father asked me for a lot of money in exchange for marrying his daughter."

"How much?"

"A lot, a great deal, Iona. A sum of money that is way beyond our means."

"And why did he do that?"

I didn't know how to answer her. Why had Hajj Salem done that? Why had he asked that crippling dowry of me and torn at the very roots of my hopes in myself?

He's rich—a millionaire, so why should he have wanted more?

But no, it's not only Hajj Salem. Mr. Seif and the merchant Omran and others—Aisha's father had done nothing new.

I don't know why, but whenever I thought of Aisha, I was beset by a feeling of pain. I loved her and still did.

It was as though Iona had read my thoughts. The smile etched on her lips vanished as she asked, "Do you still love her?"

"Yes."

Ignoring my answer, Iona turned away.

Why had I told Iona everything? Was I preparing the way to let her know my decision without realizing it?

"Did you bring me to this place to hurt me with your memories?" she said, playing with her rings. "Let's go back home. This atmosphere is killing me."

I went back to playing with my string of beads as I tried to disguise the hesitation in my voice, "Not before I tell you about my decision, the reason why I asked you to come out."

She raised her eyebrows in astonishment, "What decision?"

"We've had a good chance, Iona, to try to make things work between us, but the result doesn't really encourage us to go on. It would be better if we separated because we're not suited to each other."

When I raised my head to see the effect of my news on her, I saw that pearly tears had gathered in her eyes. Then my glance fell to her hands, which shook as though suffering the coldness of truth. I waited for her to say something, but she remained silent. After she had quickly wiped away her tears and settled her trembling hands, we returned home.

Iona entered the room quickly and I saw her gathering up all her clothes and putting them in the suitcase she had brought with her some months back.

I sat on the bed silently watching her. Reaching for the drawer, she emptied its contents onto the floor. Then she took out the kohl pencil and a small bottle of perfume and put all the other things I had bought for her back into the drawer.

Having finished, she said to me, "When can I go back to London?"

"What's the hurry?" I said, trying to calm the situation.

She didn't comment, but, clearly nervous, gave her orders, "Finish the divorce proceedings tomorrow and I'll leave."

On the following day I completed the divorce proceedings as Iona had requested and in the evening I accompanied her to the airport. Alya went with us, though my mother refused to take part in bidding Iona goodbye: she was the happiest of us all at my decision.

I heard Iona tell Alya as she was saying goodbye, "Thanks for putting me up. Your country is beautiful but I had to go back sometime to mine."

I felt sad as I watched Iona until she went up the stairs and disappeared into the plane.

When we returned home we found our mother, an expression of contentment on her face, fumigating the place as though to drive out Iona's perfume. I made my way to our room. It was empty: the stereo that had annoyed my mother so much had disappeared and the cupboard was empty of the jeans that Iona used to add to the pile of laundry.

On the stairs was a packet of cigarettes that had been carelessly thrown down, and near it a letter that Iona had written the day before to her mother and had forgotten to post.

I sat on the bed and took up the letter, which was all that was left in the house of Iona. I opened it and began to read what she had said to her mother. Her handwriting was neat and easily legible.

Dear Mother,

I am writing you this letter, having found myself with nothing to do. Even though it is nearly winter, the weather is hot. Sultan has just come back from work and has asked me to go out with him this evening.

I feel there's something he wants to talk to me about. Sultan loves children very much and enjoys playing with his auntie's boys. It seems likely that he will talk to me about having children. Sultan wants a boy, and I believe his mother would like one too, but I myself would like to have a girl.

If Sultan brings up the subject with me I shan't be able to hide the surprise from him any longer, I'll tell him I'm pregnant and he'll be delighted. Of course he'll be delighted.

Expect another letter from me full of details and give my love to Father and Mike.

Your loving daughter,
Iona

A Different Species | *Lamees Faris al-Marzuqi*

My eyes would follow her whenever she passed by our village in her little car, so unused were we to seeing a car pass through that was driven by someone other than a man. "Muna the Male" was what the village women called her. I would look at her as though she were some creature that didn't belong to the actual life we knew and lived. She was a woman unlike any other, for she didn't wear the veil as did all the married women of the village; she also didn't wear an aba, making do with a light shawl over her head. How beautiful I found her! My admiration for her would increase whenever I heard the village women talking about her in disapproving tones from which diffused fumes of jealousy whenever her small blue car passed by as she returned from work every evening. She was, in fact, the only woman in the village who had a job—yes, she was a different species of woman, and I was overcome with joy when the village women decided to pay a visit to her home.

I was longing to enter the home of the woman who was so different. My head was filled with all sorts of questions about her lifestyle and the kind of world in which she lived. How did her children feel when their mother left to go out to work? It must no doubt have felt strange to have one's mother doing a job outside the home.

I followed a group of women as they headed to her house and slipped in among them at the front door. She greeted us with a sweet smile, without any sort of covering on her head. How different she was! Her hair was short and shiny, and she had not arranged it in the way the village women do, nor had she put any henna on it so that it retained its coal-blackness.

Even her clothes were different and she wasn't wearing a jellaba. How would I feel if my own mother was like her? I tried to imagine this, but my mother's face and general appearance did not lend themselves to change, even in my imagination.

She seated us in a room round which were arranged comfortable armchairs, and I was aware of the women's whisperings as they sat down, for her house was quite unlike any of our homes. Hers resembled the homes we saw in the television serials we watched in the afternoon.

I rose from my chair to explore the beautiful house. I wandered through it and found that each corner was more beautiful than the one before, perhaps because it was a modern house and different from the traditional houses of the villagers.

She was in the kitchen with her servant, who was carrying a tray of glasses of fruit juice, and she was about to follow her out to her guests in the living room. I entered the kitchen where I found a young child seated in a chair, and I went up to her. She was no more than three years old—a beautiful child. When the servant appeared I asked her if the lady had any other children, and she replied that the family consisted of just the one little girl. A feeling of frustration enveloped me in that instant, for this child would be incapable of explaining her feelings at having a mother who was so completely unlike all other women.

A Slap in the Face | *Abdul Hamid Ahmed*

He took a taxi going to the city. He was thinking of nothing at all; in fact at one point he felt he didn't have the ability to think about anything, that he didn't have the concentration, that he wasn't seeing things properly.

He left Khor Fakkan behind him—its dryness, its dust, its rocks, its people, its sea, its sluggishness, its sun. He consoled himself during the long drive by smoking cigarettes and looking at the asphalt road and the mountains, then at the desert, with glassy, expressionless eyes. In his mouth he felt the taste of arid dryness; perhaps it was the vast desert that had brought about this feeling. He didn't know.

He stared at the driver's face and saw nothing that could move him from that idiotic state, a state like flying in a void, or staring into space, or walking on water. He didn't know.

The last time he went down to the city he had spent the evening with his friend; they had talked about everything: politics, women, the university, the electric car, the stars, and many other things. The city attracted him and he would seek it out from time to time for some reason that he couldn't quite understand, perhaps because he found in it the antithesis of the village, the beautiful village with its tranquility, dry air, poverty, laziness, friendly people, fishermen, and farmers. And the city itself is

11

very beautiful: movement, noise, unusual people, buildings, elegant shop windows, fast cars racing along asphalted roads, newspapers, books, women on the go at work in the markets. Perhaps he also liked going to the city because, from time to time, he wanted to do something to break the monotony of his days, like spending the evening out, or arguing, wandering aimlessly in streets adorned with lights, merchandise, and human beings; to attend an evening show or a lecture, to gaze at towering glass buildings instead of at the mountain begrimed with dust, or—in the best of cases—when things went right and he enjoyed a heart-warming night like the one when his friend had brought along a woman, a stranger, and he had gone to bed with her. The city's very beautiful, very spacious, very open, very free.

He went back to looking at the desert as the car approached the city. Without knowing why, he found himself asking the driver, "Friend, Khor Fakkan better? Dubai better?"

"Khor Fakkan have good air, good mountain. Dubai have much work, much money."

Then, having opened the window and spat out of it, he continued, saying, "Emirates all good."

He fell silent, though the short conversation with the driver had opened a fresh appetite for thought. What did people do in the city? Very many things; everything was available. The state of reflection began to fall away and to be replaced by one of questioning and inquiry.

In Khor Fakkan life was ordinary, days monotonous, the same work repeated day after day. The fishermen and farmers, how friendly they were! They would talk to him about their concerns, even their private ones, their very private ones like their relationships with their wives. How splendid they were in their frankness! The city had other things, things more beautiful;

people there thought in a way that was different from that of the villagers, they were cultured.

He came to a stop at the final word, repeating it to himself. It became a big question in need of an answer, an answer of any kind. But of what kind? He didn't know, except that the city was most certainly beautiful, very beautiful.

Tonight he would discuss this very same point with his friend. Each time he went to the city, any city, be it Abu Dhabi, Dubai, Sharjah or some other, he discovered something new. Once, he had said to his friend that when he went to the city it was as if he were invading it, exploring it, and they had talked about this for a long time.

On arrival in Dubai he went to his friend's house. It was around four o'clock and he didn't find him at home. He walked around for a while: his friend wouldn't come before eight in the evening. Strolling round the streets is a real pleasure.

He looked at the shops, crossed streets, stood still on pavements, smoked cigarettes, watched people going and coming, observed women. He thought: Here women alone are worthy of being watched, of being glanced at furtively. In Khor Fakkan women were all wrapped up and veiled, both indoors and out. Talking to them was extraordinarily difficult. Here things were different: a woman wears a beautiful dress, she goes out shopping, she engages in conversation. Dresses, shapes, and sizes, different hairdos: this one is white, that a dark Indian, a blonde, English or Dutch; this one an Egyptian or Lebanese. A local girl raises her flimsy aba above her bottom. A pleasure, merely looking is a pleasure here. Then there's . . . . He stopped thinking. "What?" he said to himself. "What about asking something of one of them? She might say yes and she might say no. What's it matter? It's up to her, and I have nothing to lose."

Before crossing the street, he turned left and right. His dishdasha wasn't as clean as it might have been, and he was hatless. No one was paying him any attention; people passed around him, in front and behind, men and women, while he stayed rooted to the pavement: pristine cars, magnificent shops, lights. What beauty! He caught sight of a woman on the other pavement. He crossed over behind her and followed her. His cold glances caught up with her: two well-formed legs as pure as milk, and a bottom that went well with the tall body. She was walking on her own.

He came to a stop in front of a shop window. He stood about two meters from her. He stared at her: she was beautiful, very beautiful. City women are beautiful like the cities themselves, civilized like the cities themselves. She walked on, he walked on; she came to a stop, he came to a stop. She bent down to adjust her shoe. Her bottom turned around; he was greatly taken by the sight of it. She walked on. Should he continue to follow after her? He didn't trouble to answer. He walked on. She stopped at a goldsmith's shop window. He drew close. Standing alongside her, he began staring at the shop window, his body almost touching hers. He breathed in the delicious perfume. She might say yes and she might say no.

"Excuse me, would it be possible for you to have sex with me?"

She raised her head, her eyes darting about and filled with astonishment, embarrassment, or indecision, he didn't know which. Open-mouthed, she stared at him. Had the question baffled her? He stood there as cool as a statue, his eyes evincing nothing. He stared back at her: she was certainly beautiful. He waited. "Yes . . . no." One of the two words. She too continued to stare. It seemed she either didn't believe what she'd heard or she hadn't heard it. She had in fact heard it but didn't want to believe it, or else she didn't believe what she had heard. Had he said something unbelievable? He didn't know. She remained still. Gently he repeated, "Is it possible that . . . ? I believe you heard. Just say yes or no. It's as you like."

Her face flushed red and her lips gaped open as she let out a horrific scream. She gave out a howl and seized him by the collar.

"What are you saying?" she screamed. "You good-for-nothing scum! The man's crazy!"

He tried to say something. Did his words merit all this screaming and wailing? Before he could open his mouth he found himself surrounded by a crowd of people, among them a policeman. The latter intervened.

"You insolent good-for-nothing!"

He remained silent and the policeman took the two of them to the police station.

As she continued to shout curses and abuse, he remained silent and calm, as though nothing had happened. Had anything happened? He didn't know, but it was no doubt an adventure. It could be explained with humor or regret, or with tears, or a fresh investigation!

At the station he found himself alone with the officer.

"What's your name?"

"Said Abdullah."

"Age?"

"Twenty."

"What's your job?"

"A student at university."

"Why did you do this?"

"What did I do?"

"How can you bring yourself to assault people?"

"I didn't assault anyone," he replied coolly.

"You spoke improperly to the lady," said the officer.

"I may have said something, but I didn't do anything. Anyway, what I said wasn't, as you say, improper."

"You made an unseemly proposition to her."

He answered calmly, "I proposed something to her that she could accept or reject as she thought fit—she's free. Instead, she flew into a rage and made an unnecessary fuss."

"What?" said the officer, open-mouthed.

"It was assumed that she would accept what I suggested, but she had the right to accept or refuse. She's free."

The officer gave an audible groan.

"But you're not free to do as you wish," he said angrily.

"What?" said Said in astonishment. "She's free and I'm free. I have the right to ask for something I want, and she has the right to accept or refuse calmly; there's no need for all this fuss."

Said was silent for a while—what was he to say? It was a dispute that was utterly senseless, but continuing with it was enjoyable. There was definitely something wrong somewhere. No doubt about that!

"You're a student," said the officer, "and you must observe common manners. Haven't you learned that at school?"

"I learned other things too." Then he continued confidently, "Haven't you heard of democracy?"

The officer became aflame with rage.

"Are you going to become ill-mannered here too?"

"We're discussing things calmly, why the anger? You have the right to answer me, to discuss the matter with me."

"We aren't here to have a discussion. We're talking about the case with which you are charged. You acted unlawfully toward the lady."

"I did nothing of the kind," Said interrupted him. "I didn't touch her, I didn't hit her, I didn't rape her. I asked her a question to which I did not receive an answer. All I heard was screaming. It had nothing to do with it. It's not, as I believe, a matter for anger."

The officer's eyes widened, "You ask a woman you don't know something like that and then say it's not something to get angry about!"

"And she, too, doesn't know me. She could simply have said no and gone her way in peace. I exercised my democratic right, but she . . . ."

"Shut up!" the officer interrupted him with increased anger.

"She could have said something but she didn't exercise her democratic right. She shouted, creating a difficulty out of nothing. It's my right to ask and hers to refuse. In Europe a young man says what he wishes to a girl. That's freedom—there isn't any question of assault."

"Excuse me, allow me to say something," said the officer. "What would you like to add?" he added, this time sarcastically.

"What I said is correct: she didn't exercise her right—all she did was scream and get angry. Had she just said 'No,' I'd have let her be and walked off. That's all it's about."

"You're immature, crazy!"

"I'm not immature—it's just that you don't want to understand. You become upset right away and get angry. What do you want of me now?"

"That you come to your senses—nothing more." Then he added sternly, "The punishment in such a case is a day in prison, unless the lady waives her rights."

"A punishment for something I didn't do."

The officer ignored him and called the policeman to bring in the lady. Said kept his silence.

As she entered, Said eyed her, saying to himself: There's no doubt she's beautiful, very beautiful.

"What do you want to do now? As you can see, he's a young adolescent; you can either forgive him or we can punish him with a night and a day in prison."

Said looked at her. "Why did you scream? If you'd kept quiet, if you'd said 'No,' neither you nor I would have come here and all this wouldn't have happened."

"You're insolent . . . insolent." Then she continued, "No, I'll not forgive him. I want to slap him on the face—right now!"

"Why?" exclaimed Said in astonishment.

"Let's put a stop to this nonsense," said the officer. "I agree to your request."

The policeman took hold of Said and the woman came up to him and slapped him a couple of times on the face. While having a sensation of great heat in his cheeks, Said screamed at her, "You're stupid, crazy . . . you're really stupid."

Said spent the night and a day in the prison of the police station. When he got out, night had fallen and lights were shining from high up in the buildings and along the roads. The city was beautiful in its splendid new garb. But this time it did not tempt him. How had all this happened? He restrained a bitter laugh inside himself: should he go to his friend and tell him exactly what had happened? No, he would laugh and make fun of the incident, he would regard it as madness. Hadn't the stupid woman given him a couple of slaps?

He stopped a taxi.

"Khor Fakkan, please."

The taxi sped along with him into the night across the desert, leaving behind the city with its hubbub and uproar, its residents in all their finery, their fast cars and fancy watches, their captivating perfumes emanating from their clothes, their whole appearance signifying luxury. There was nothing in his head to think about, although he felt, as he touched the part of his face that had been slapped, that it was the city that had slapped him hard so unexpectedly and that it resembled the woman he had spoken to: beautiful but vacuous, possessed of nothing except for a foolhardy scream.

Abu Abboud

Ali Abdul Aziz al-Sharhan

In a corner of his humble room in one of the workers' dwellings his family had obtained from the federal government, Abu Abboud sat sprawled out on the mat he had refused to leave behind in his old house made of palm fronds. He had not moved to this room of his own free will, despite his happiness and knowledge that the family enjoyed stability there. This had given him the kind of peace of mind about the future that he had long dreamed of and for which he had sacrificed all his youth. It had been his sole aim in life to provide security and ease for his children and grandchildren. His feeble body was relaxing on one of the cushions fashioned by the hands of that old woman who had breathed her last and whom he had buried a year ago when she lost her life in a car accident on the road close to the present house. At this moment his eyes roved over the whole room, among the objects scattered about and hung in all four quarters until his eyes came to rest on the nose-peg that he had used when he was a pearl diver some quarter of a century ago.

"May God punish you, O time—you took all the days of my youth and squandered them on pearl diving at sea. We don't know how they passed. In those days we suffered such distress, fatigue, and grief, days when one didn't taste any rest or happiness. We would spend four months at sea, diving in the dark shallows, in

search of a mere morsel of bread and enduring curses and abuse
from the ship's captain. All that trouble evaporates when you get
back to this homeland that contains our wives and our past and
for which we have given our very souls."

These thoughts of Abu Abboud evoked others from his pearl
diving days and of his youth, and he began to talk. It was as
though he were relating a story in which he was the hero, a
story of those who had lived those days and undergone the same
suffering. Abu Abboud continued to talk of things that were filled
with anguish, memories of days past, a record of the history of
his ancestors, of stories that gave clear proof of the greatness of
those men who had spared no effort to become examples to the
generation that now lived on in their memory and enjoyed the
good things of life that they had defended.

"Where are those days about which one could fill more than
a million pages and books? The sea—both friend and a foe—
how many men perished in its waters, and how many men
became slaves to debt, and how many of them made orphans
of their children?

"Along the whole of this coast that has now become a country
there was a small village that scraped a living from what the
sea provided. No one thought of having more than what was
necessary to provide his children with something to fill their
bellies and a house to protect them from the winter's cold. I,
this old man, was born in the year just before the famine that
came upon us. During that year there was hunger all along the
coast, no food of any kind to be found, with people dying in the
streets from hunger, and with no one escaping this fate other
than those who had stored away some dates. I grew up in our
house made of palm fronds that my father had built by himself.
In those days I was still young and was tethered with a rope
inside the tent so that I couldn't play in the dirt—my favorite

pastime. Days passed and I began to understand and realize what was happening before my eyes. My father was a fisherman but he didn't own the necessary equipment and so would go with our neighbor Abu Khalaf, who had a Shahuf boat and the wire baskets that were used for fishing and was thus a man of wealth. Abu Khalaf was not liked by others, for he was a greedy man and would torment my father. What upset me most was when I saw him humiliating my father when he refused to go fishing with him. And what made me hate him even more was when he would knock at the tent in the middle of the night and call out to my father to tell him that it was time to go out to sea. His voice would make me jump up from my sleep, interrupting the lovely dreams I was having. In the spring when the sea was calm and the sky blue, I stood one day on the shore waiting for my father to carry for him the fish he had got from the grasping Abu Khalaf. We arrived at the house with me carrying the basket made from palm fronds holding my father's share of the fish, an amount that would barely feed two people. At the door of our house my mother was waiting for us, happy at the return of my father from the sea, for she knew only too well that the sea was fraught with difficulties, fatigue, and dangers. No sooner did afternoon come on that particular day than my father was lying in bed shivering from a high fever. In tears, my mother sent me to Umm Mohamed who lived at the top end of the village to ask her to send her husband to treat my father by cauterizing him. What I remember is that Umm Mohamed and her husband had a place for treating people by cauterizing them. Having reached the house, Abu Mohamed, the husband, went in to where my father was covered up and groaning with pain. A while later they brought the fire and put a large nail in it. I couldn't bear to watch the scene and I went on crying for my father, frightened about the fire they were going to burn him with.

"He remained in that state for many days, unable to go to sea or even to move, and all the while we had nothing to eat. Every day Abu Khalaf would knock at our door and ask about my father, wanting him to go to sea; if he didn't go, he said, he would sack him.

"A year, two years, and then a third passed with my father still bedridden and us getting into debt with Abu Khalaf, who wanted me to take my father's place. But my mother would refuse him. Then things got worse for my father and he died. My eyes filled with tears as I wept at being separated from him. I wept, too, for the circumstances in which we would be living from then on. What could I do at that age, with me no more than fifteen and with my mother refusing Abu Khalaf's request that I work with him, and with Abu Khalaf threatening me about the debts we had run up? After that I decided to work with him. Then once, coming back from sea, I saw my mother standing as usual by the door waiting for me, and she smiled when she saw me, but I didn't know why. When I asked her she said that Ibrahim the boat captain, who had a boum dhow that was making the trip to India and the East African coast, wanted me to go with him as a boy to work the small dingy in which passengers were taken out to the dhow. When I heard the news I was overjoyed and felt that I had grown up and now had taken on many responsibilities. And best of all, I would enjoy being at sea and visiting different countries, but when I looked at my mother standing close by me, I saw tears flowing down her cheeks because of the pain she felt at being separated from me. I realized that the separation would be difficult for her, she being alone in this world, but that this was her fate."

A few moments went by with Abu Abboud still in deep thought about the past and the effect on him of painful memories. A hot tear slipped down his lined cheek and into his mouth, its salty taste reminding him of the drops of sweat that made their way to his mouth while at work. With the coming of night, darkness took over, with Abu Abboud seated motionless, for he was used to the darkness when it penetrated the very depths between the coral rocks as he searched for the shells in which lay the pearls that were the source of his livelihood. Those were days that had had their place in the long life of Abu Abboud.

A knocking at the door awakens him from his thoughts of when he was the son who would listen to his own father talk to him of days long ago. His conversation had been enthralling for a son whose only link to the world in which his father had lived had been memory, a world that had become like a fairy tale to be told whenever people were gathered together.

"Good evening, Father."

"Good evening, Salem."

"How are you today, Father?"

"I'm fine. Where have you been? You were nowhere to be seen all this time. You still don't stop playing around and staying up late. How many times have I advised you that there's nothing good about this world of ours? I want you to pay attention to your studies because the coming days will have no mercy. As your father, I'm telling you that nothing but knowledge is going to be of any benefit to you."

"Father, I'm bored with studying. I want to go out to work and get married and have some nice young girl born to me who will look after you."

"Listen to me—I'm your father, I want you to finish your studies and get a diploma that will keep my head high among people."

"Oh, I go on and on studying. I see all those who have studied who haven't got anywhere. I know lots of those who haven't studied who are now becoming rich."

"My boy, give up thinking that way. You must learn and find yourself a place and a job and assure your children a better future."

"Listen, father, don't go on. I don't want to study."

"Salem my boy, I don't have that much more time to live and I want you to pursue the dreams I've lived for all my life."

Birds of a Feather | *Jumaa al-Fairuz*

bu Amani was thirty-five years of age, of medium height, burly, and had a sallow complexion. He worked at one of the local government offices and lived with his mother and brothers in an old house in one of the residential quarters. He hadn't married and was frightened of the idea and lived a strange, unsettled life. As for women, he paid them no heed, though he pretended to his friends, who would come to his house every night, that he knew everything about them. He had never known a woman in his life, with one exception: the woman who had a house opposite him and lived with her husband in one of the other emirates and who would every now and again return to her old house. During her time there Abu Amani would meet up with her several times. His friends would say of him that had he known women—as he claimed—he would have ventured into marriage, and the wife would have played the same part in his life that drinking and smoking, which he indulged in every night, did at present.

He was a man of weak character, having no opinions of his own and following any opinion expressed by one of his friends. He liked reading and was keen to own books, which he would line up, covered in dust, in his bedroom and in the lounge. He liked to pretend to his friends that he was a man of culture, but they would say behind his back that he didn't read a single line of these books, and that he only kept them because he liked to show off. All he read were the novels of Arsene Lupin and Agatha Christie and some children's magazines like *Superman* and *Tintin*. He would meet his friends in the lounge, which included a desk and chair and rows of the books for which there was no room in the small dust-covered library.

Every night he would stay up until dawn then go off to his work, drawn and haggard. He would hardly spend an hour in the office before leaving it and making his way back home in order to sleep until evening. Because he'd worked in the same department for a long time and was from the same town, they were unable to sack him. However, when they had tired of his long absences from work they transferred him to a job where he could attend when he wished and go home when he wished.

Often he would claim to his friends, the regular visitors to his house, that he was paid bonuses for his efficiency at work, and he would display the bank notes that he had with him, which sums came either from the inheritance from his father or from the woman neighbor, who would give him money whenever she came on her usual holidays. She never begrudged him anything, always giving him money and presents, which she would bring with her because in the days when she had been poor he had been kind to her. His friends knew that he was lying, that he didn't go to work at the office and was not given any bonuses but was spending his days asleep. However, they listened to him in silence as though they believed him, but on leaving they would express a very different view of him. These friends were all sorts: workers, government employees, and vagabonds without work or a place to live, who would spend their evenings with him, smoking cigarettes, drinking whiskey, and chatting about trivial matters right through the night. Among them were sheikhs who professed to be Sufis, men who spent their whole lives going from one mosque to another, but they were no different than Abu Amani in their behavior, and they would say that there was nothing wrong with him.

Abu Amani would tell all his acquaintances that it was he who spent on his friends, that they ate, drank, and smoked cigarettes at his expense, while they, in turn, maintained that each one of them paid for himself, but that they had no other place than his home in which they could meet away from prying eyes. But Abu Amani loved to play the part of the moneyed man who looked after those he knew. When he was in need of some money, he would regard nothing as precious, selling off some of his possessions at the cheapest of prices. Each month his room would see a change: things would appear, others would disappear. A lot would disappear. A stereo would make materialize and then disappear, likewise a television set and a radio. His drunken friends would gather around him and regard the set with wonderment, while he would stand by with a supercilious look on his face. Their evening sessions would sometimes last until morning, when they would disperse, some going home to sleep, others seeking somewhere on the pavements. Still others would go off to work, returning home after an hour. Abu Amani would take himself to his bed so as to sleep the whole day through in preparation for yet another festive night.

One of his most beloved friends was Hajj Ali, a man of about fifty-five who wore a tattered dishdasha and a turban. He gave the impression of being someone who was confused, idiotic even, though sometimes he could come across as malicious and wily. Abu Amani claimed that Hajj Ali was a famous lawyer with a house, a wife, and children but that he had become a Sufi and had devoted himself to the love of God, spending his days moving between the mosques frequented by the Sufis, one day being in the al-Batah Mosque and another in the big mosque in the souk. He was forever moving about between the various quarters and villages to hear the sermons of the imams and those with knowledge of God. He also claimed that Hajj Ali had performed miracles that he himself had witnessed, for he would reach his hand into the tattered pocket of his dishdasha and produce bank notes that he would give to those in need without being asked.

One day he arrived from a faraway country and went into Abu Amani's room, saying that he had come especially on his account. Abu Amani was sitting on the chair and the Hajj on the edge of the bed when the Hajj said to him, "Come along, Abu Amani. I want you to come here."

Abu Amani left his chair and sat himself beside Hajj on the bed. No sooner had he sat down than a lump of masonry fell down from the roof onto the place where he had just been sitting. It consisted of large chunks of stone, quite capable of killing him had they fallen on his head. Abu Amani looked at the chunks of stone in terror and disbelief. Then he became aware that the Hajj was talking to him, "I've got to go now—I have many things to do. I have done what I had to do here. Till we meet again soon."

Abu Amani took hold of the Hajj's hand and began kissing it.

"May God bless you and lengthen your life," he told him. "You saved me from certain death."

Abu Amani recounted this incident to his friends and acquaintances. The place where the pieces of masonry had fallen from the roof could clearly be seen right above the chair.

From this day on Abu Amani's regard for Hajj Ali grew until it reached one of veneration, such was the esteem in which he held him. He would prepare the finest of foods for him whenever he visited, slaughtering local chickens and thrusting a handful of bank notes into Hajj Ali's pocket just as he was leaving. Abu

Amani would tell of another of Hajj Ali's miracles. At al-Batah
Mosque he went with Hajj Ali and some of his friends to the rank
for taxis going to Dubai. The rank was crowded with people and
when one of the taxis came they all climbed into it, all except Hajj
Ali. When one of them tried to give up his place to Hajj Ali, the
Hajj ordered him to stay where he was—and none of us would
think of disobeying an order from him. So the taxi sped off with
them to Dubai; then, right in front of the door of the mosque in
one of the city's residential quarters they found Hajj Ali standing
there waiting for them. No sooner did they see him than they
shouted out with joy, not believing their eyes. One of them asked
his companion in wonder, "How did the Hajj get here before us?
We left him standing at the taxi rank in Ras al-Khaima."

"The Hajj has powers of his own. In a single step he arrived
here in Dubai. The Hajj is a great spiritual leader."

Then, one evening, the Hajj came to pay Abu Amani a visit.
No sooner had he seated himself than he said, "Mr. Abu Amani,
I have come from Bahrain especially to see you."

Abu Amani was overjoyed.

"This is a great honor, my Lord Sheikh. Are you coming just
for me from that distant place?"

Taking hold of Abu Amani's hands and patting them, the
Hajj said, "Listen, Abu Amani, I've come because of something
important that concerns you. A girl—she doesn't know you and
you don't know her—has seen you in a dream. She has seen
you just as you are and with your name. She came to me so that
I might explain her dream for her. I was not surprised, for such
things are part of the supernatural that we do not know about."

Abu Amani's interest was aroused by the Hajj's words. "Speak,
O Lord Sheikh, for I am anxious to learn about this news."

The Hajj told him, "The girl told me that she had seen a young
man in the dream wearing a white dishdasha. She described the

young man to me and I saw that it was you. The young man had said to her, 'My name is Abu Amani and I have come to ask for your hand in marriage from your family.' Thus has it been written in the tablet of fate."

Abu Amani was extremely surprised by these words. "How extraordinary, O Sheikh!" he told the Hajj in a daze.

"Listen here, Abu Amani," the Hajj told him. "This is the wife that was decreed for you in the unseen. With her there will be happiness, so don't hesitate—let's go to her."

With growing surprise Abu Amani said, "Now, my Lord Sheikh? This very night?"

"Now, without a moment's delay. Who knows what will happen tomorrow. The young man she saw in the dream said to her, 'My name is Abu Amani Mohamed.' That's your full name. Do you want better proof that happiness awaits you with this young girl?"

Within minutes Abu Amani had put on his dishdasha and gone out with the sheikh to the airport, and so to Bahrain. They arrived at seven-thirty in the morning and took a taxi. As the taxi was approaching a small village whose new buildings had scarcely made their presence felt, the sheikh ordered the driver to stop. They then got out of the taxi, with Abu Amani asking himself, "How did the Hajj know which village it was when there were tens of villages along the way?"

Suddenly they heard barking and they were surrounded by dogs that were about to tear them to pieces, but the sheikh quietly addressed them, "Off with you, each to its house. Go away!"

The dogs stopped barking and stood there in silence. Abu Amani, who had been shaking with fear, couldn't believe what had happened. The dogs gradually took off and disappeared among the trees. The two men entered one of the village houses and were warmly received. The owner of the house bent over the

Hajj's hand and went on kissing it for a long time. The man was
the girl's father. A few moments later food was produced and
presented to the two guests.

The Hajj said to the man, "This is Mr. Abu Amani. He's an
important government official and I have brought him here to be
a bridegroom for your daughter."

"Could I refuse a request from you, Lord Sheikh? Your every
request is obeyed."

The girl entered, greeted the two men, and retired. She was a
prodigy of captivating rural beauty.

The opening chapter of the Koran was recited to seal the
marriage, and Abu Amani went off to take his afternoon nap, the
happiest of God's creatures. On the following day the two were
married and the girl went back with Abu Amani as his wife, with
Sheikh Ali accompanying them. The lounge was turned into a
bedroom for the sheikh, with a bed, a pillow, and a prayer rug,
and the man was left on his own.

When Abu Amani consummated the marriage and discovered
that his bride wasn't a virgin, he didn't sleep the whole night and
remained seated in his chair as he smoked with bowed head. As
for the girl she didn't stop crying and uttered not a word. In the
morning a pale and trembling Abu Amani went to see the sheikh
and told him frankly what had happened. The sheikh lowered his
head for a time. There was a deep silence, then he raised his head
and quietly said, "O Abu Amani, don't resist. This is your fate,
so be content with it and forgive."

Abu Amani was unable to reply. He kept silent and lowered
his head in thought. Listening to his sheikh's advice, he pardoned
and forgave, and kept his secret buried deep inside him.

The days passed with Abu Amani leading a happy married
life, though he didn't give up his friends or stop spending his
every evenings with them. Sheikh Ali would, as was his habit,

pay him visits every now and again and was met as ever with open arms and respect. The wife would kiss his hand and ask him to pray that she might have good fortune and her husband divine guidance and piety. Two years passed, but Abu Amani did not become a father. One day he raised the subject with the sheikh, "Good sir, two years have gone by and no child has been born to me. I love children so much and was so hoping to have a child who would fill my life. What's happened to your prayers and miracles?"

The sheikh lowered his head in thought, then said, "I shall go to the souk to buy some incense and shall come back. At night the sheikh returned and asked Abu Amani to prepare him an incense burner, and the scent of the incense was discharged into the bedroom. The wife came and seated herself in front of him and he asked Abu Amani to leave them on their own and not to put on any light in the house so that he might scent the wife with incense and recite over her some blessings and incantations.

The smoke from the incense permeated the room from beneath the door, filling the whole house with its fragrance. When al-Hajj called out to Abu Amani, who was squatting by the window in the living room looking out at the street, he patted him on the shoulder with the words, "All in due time, Abu Amani, so don't rush things."

Abu Amani lived his whole life without having children, finally coming to realize that he had been duped.

Death

Omniyat Salem

On that day my father came with traces of tears in his eyes. It was the first time I had ever seen him cry. My father crying, crying behind me. I heard him telling my mother that he had buried her, that she had died and was at peace. It was his mother. All I see is blackness. "What does the death of his parents mean?" "Where has she gone?" "They say she's with her Lord."

"Her lord is that mosque over there."

"No, her Lord is God who created us and made us whole, and after all this hardship we return to Him." He cried silently.

That silent tortured soul who lived an isolation of his own choosing. I didn't know that he loved someone more than me. Whenever that woman had seen me she had put me into the bath to wash me. I would escape from her and run toward the sea, their loyal neighbor on that island. I would see strange-looking birds standing on the shore and gazing at me. I would hear a small boy singing and chasing the birds, "We're Zaab Muslims . . . hostile . . . I sang it . . . We're Zaab Muslims. . . ."

They laughed, my aunts, and my father, and mother. My grandmother laughed. I repeated it to her. My father took me by the hand and wandered around with me all through the island. He said, "This is my grandfather's big house, and this, my uncle's house, the house of the uncle who brought me up. And here is where my grandfather's wife used to live." The houses were changed to addresses and images that were inscribed with words that defined them. Their inhabitants were in his memory. Every place had its own special memory for him. Every house had a story and a meaning. "Over there,"—and he pointed far off. I used to go to al-Mukhalleen Naqeez. It was an inhabited area. Whenever we came to sleep we'd hear, outside, a she-wolf crying out, "My children . . . my children," and a shudder would shoot through my body. I'd ask him, "Do wolves know how to talk?" and he'd reply, "No, it was a female djinn. Her children have died and she cries for them every night." Do djinn know how to cry? What do they look like? He doesn't answer. The questions I put to him were mere chatter. His distractedness sent him faraway while his hand continued to hold mine. I tried to free myself from him. His grip slackened and gave reins to my feelings of wanting to be free, to go off as I please. He recited to me the Chapter of the Djinn from the Koran, then told me story after story. I arrived with him at Umm al-Duwais's house, the woman who went out every night all made up and perfumed in order to seduce men. At that moment I thanked God that I was not a man. My father laughed. I asked him, "Is it quite certain she doesn't like girls? Then I'd not be a tasty quarry for her." Her story has always been surrounded with secrets, queries, hidden worlds. She isn't so much an amusing story as a tragedy and a mystery, and suspicion attaches itself to a woman who goes out like that, all dressed up after the sunset prayers. It is as though, with these tales being a mixture of fantasy and real life, people have their doubts about a woman who leaves her home after darkness. What does darkness mean other than that thick, striking blackness, like a magic moving aba with a sort of foam towering over it? No one knows darkness as do the people of the sea and the desert: cold, black, cruel sands, and a strange black wave, as though desert and sky were twins separated by an imaginary line like the line of the equator. With the darkness not leaving my bedroom, I fled to my father to sleep in his lap and hide myself with him in the bed and to listen to his sweet-sounding breathing as though it were a fence protecting me from what might happen were I to sit out in the open.

From that time on my father became unhappy. A look of bewilderment, as if he had strayed into matters he didn't quite comprehend never left his face. That look became a permanent feature after his mother bade him farewell and gave him no promise of return. That unhappy, long-suffering Muslim.

I scratched his back for him to make him laugh. I sat on his back so he could relax. I told him about my adventures—the last of them was when I went into my grandmother's when she was in the bath. He smiled. "Shame on you," he said. I answered him, "I didn't know." She'd also said to me, "Shame on you. Get out of here, you with the blackened face!" My face was white, so why did she tell me it's black? I sat down angrily, thinking about how a face could be black. I prayed to God for it not to happen. I asked him, "Will my face become as black as our neighbor Amal?" He said, "No." He handed me half a dirham and said, "Buy yourself some ice cream." At this I see myself as owning the whole world and my eyes shone with a magical glitter at this treasure in the palm of my hand. Quickly, barefoot, I ran to the shop. Someone smiled at me, called to me. I ignored him. He provoked me by saying, "What's that boy's clothing you're wearing?" I came to a stop and looked at him, with my hand around my waist, mocking him, "I like what I'm wearing and I don't like your face." He guffawed with laughter. Nothing worried me—the only thing of importance was the treasure hidden away in the palm of my hand and what I'd be doing with it. I entered a shop with a door as blue as the sea. "Where's Mamoo?" I asked the man. Abu Bakr replied, "What do you want of Mamoo—he's gone off to the souk." I grasped this glass that embraced frozen milk; I kissed it and sat down to savor it at my leisure. I heard someone calling me. It was the old lady, our neighbor, who had sat down to have a rest. "Mama Moza, is there something you want?" "No," she said. "I sewed this for your mother and I'm going to your house." She was wearing thick glasses and a long veil. She walked slowly and I overtook her. I held her bits and pieces, and from time to time I stumbled, so that the ice cream fell to the sand. I looked at it tearfully and hurriedly threw down the old woman's things at the door and sneaked into my father's arms while fighting against the sobbing lament for that heavy loss!

Enemies in a Single House

Maryam Jumaa Faraj

We hadn't left the house for days and I was unable to count the things it had in it. There was water, lots of it. My grandmother put her hand into the can of dates, filling it and pounding them.

"Watch the date palm," she said to me.

"Why?"

"When the date palm dies we'll know everything."

"How's that?"

"All the ripe dates will fall down from it; when the date palms waste away, the war will start. That's what they say."

"Who?"

"Everyone."

"If the date palm dies, what will we do?"

"We'll stay in the house or we'll flee."

"Where to?"

"Oh, to the desert."

"To the land," said I.

"Yes," she answered.

My grandmother filled the can with dates and we dragged out the can in which there was the dried fish.

"And tomorrow we'll grind the little fishes," said my grandmother. "If God gives us life." I hadn't talked with my grandmother very much, though she began telling me stories about the war in the days of old, the days of the war of the Christians, and I was frightened and she was telling me songs of war.

She was saying, "The old warriors would say to the war, 'We are devils and Satans of war,' just as the warrior Antara ibn Shaddad used to do."

My father came in. He had with him a sack of sand and another one full of wood. After he had put them down in the courtyard I think he went off to listen to the radio.

"This is your father," said my blind grandmother.

"Yes, grandma, he's come from the mosque."

"No, he's come from the land," she said.

"Who told you?"

"The way he smells. He came with wood for the stove."

"Yes."

"And he brought gas."

"Yes, Grandma," I answered testily.

Said my grandmother, pointing at the stove, "Look—over there."

"What's over there?"

"Seven cats."

"Where?"

"Hung up."

"Hung up where?"

"In the stove . . . and the stove's in need of wood, and the wood is from the samra tree, and the samra tree needs an axe, and the axe is with the woodcutter."

I knew then that she was quoting a song and I went on repeating it with her, the song of the seven cats, in my high-pitched voice. But she stopped and said, "Now what shall we do?"

"Now we'll go to the samra tree," I told her.

"Now," she said. "We can't now, there's a war on."

"Yes, Grandma."

She was making fun of me.

"If the war starts," I asked her, "what are we going to eat?"

"We'll eat tuna and dates and dry bread."

"I don't like tuna," I said to her.

"And I don't like dry bread," she said. "No one likes tuna, and no one likes dry bread, and no one likes war."

"Why?" I asked her.

"In times of war people have died of hunger and they've shrouded them in sacking and buried them."

"Then I don't like war."

"Hush," she said to me.

When she fell silent I heard their quarrelling once again.

"They'll win," said my father.

"They won't win," said my mother.

"They're the strongest," said my father.

"I don't believe so," said my mother.

"That's how it is," said my father.

"Let the world go up in flames!" said my mother.

"And what have we done wrong?" said my father.

My grandmother wept and so did my mother, and my father stayed on by himself with the radio, while also watching the television.

"What will they do with us?" said my grandmother.

I imagined them to be mere steps away from us.

My father and mother were quarrelling, and my grandmother pronounced, "I bear witness there is no god but God. Ask them both when the war's going to happen."

I got the impression they'd patched it up.

However I asked him, "What's war, father?"

He was silent, then drew close. "Let's try out war," he said, making fun.

"We must turn out the lights," he said. "And we must divide ourselves into two groups. One group is with me and the other is with your mother. Fahd goes with your mother, and Jassim with you and me," said my father to me.

At this I felt perplexed and didn't answer, and I went to stand between the two of them.

"And your grandmother—she's old," he said, "and all she can do is watch."

My granny didn't hear a thing.

"Who among us is the owner of the house, and who's the stranger?" he said.

"I," said my mother, "it's I who am the owner of the house."

"No, it's I who am the owner of the house," said my father.

My father flew into a rage and so did my mother. The two of them talked in loud voices and advanced on one another . . . .

When they came close to one another, I could hear their breathing. It was as if one of them was going to kill the other.

Fear Without Walls

'A'ishaa al-Za'aby

A ll the paths into that poor district led to that abandoned house perched on a small elevated plot of land. No one remembers exactly when the building was put up, a building whose doors and windows had become playthings for the winds, and most of the old people agreed that it had been there before they were born or even before their mothers were born. But the story of that house and the multitude of tales that surrounded it had given it a certain importance, even though it had become little more than a subject of gossip for old women and those with nothing to do when they met up. At times like that, each woman would add something new of her own and swear by all that was holy that it was true, so much so that the listener would begin to have doubts about the tale. That mansion, as it was called, brought on everyone who lived in it, or even went near it, a curse that was like that of the pharaohs.

Let us go back a few years and journey along the route of the account of the oldest inhabitant of this simple quarter, an account that tells the tale of a house with three generations of people who lived in it. That old man says, "Among the things my father told me about the house is that it was owned by a cloth merchant who had no one to leave it to apart from an only daughter and an old servant woman who took care of the daughter after the death of her mother. The daughter had become greatly attached to the servant, so much so that she would secretly call her 'mother.' The young girl was living on her own because her father the merchant prevented her from mixing with the simple locals, arguing that by doing so she might catch some of the chronic diseases to which they were suspect. The girl submitted to such orders, though she would watch the children of the quarter at their games, and follow their comings and goings from the enclosed window of her room.

"One night, screams were heard from the house, which had come to be known as the 'cemetery of silence' because of its utter soundlessness. Many of the village inhabitants rushed out to enquire about the source of the horrible screams and were quickly guided to where they came from, for the screaming continued unabated, stirring in people's minds the most ghastly horrors that could be imagined.

"A group of men and women reached that gloomy house and were just approaching the courtyard when the lamps they were carrying lit up a horrific scene, the memory of which still brings a shudder akin to that of the tremor of death to all those who had seen it. The father was heaping earth upon his head without realizing what he was doing as he screamed and raved deliriously, while alongside him lay the body of the old servant woman, her unrecognizable, severed limbs scattered around as though they had fallen prey to the fangs of hungry lions. The simple villagers stood dazed without moving, and at the time nothing could be heard except for the howling of the stricken father who was muttering disconnected words, 'My daughter . . . she's disappeared . . . my daughter . . . lost . . . my daughter . . . my daughter. . . .' after which he fell motionless to the ground and his voice was stilled for ever. No one in the group dared to draw close to her, or even to leave the place. They remained where they were until the sun rose the next day to shed its light on that terrible scene. It was then that some of the men began to move and circle around the two corpses. They started to ask each other what possibly could have happened in that ill-fated house, and to wonder where that girl they had so often seen watching them from her window had disappeared to.

"Some of them entered the house and searched around, but they found no trace of her. They looked into every nook and cranny of the small village but it was like looking for a grain of sand that the winds had swept away.

"The inhabitants of the village buried the corpse of the ill-fated father and that of the poor servant woman, then went back to their homes and jobs, unable to forget that there was certainly a terrible secret behind this tragedy, and asking themselves where the girl could be and what could have happened to her.

"The simple villagers went on weaving story after story about the possible outcome of that terrible night. Some of them came up with the idea that ghosts had invaded the house, driving out its inhabitants in that horrible manner and that they had abducted the young girl. Others said that there had to be a gang of wicked people behind what had happened. And so the stories went on being fabricated and woven together. But all the theories, both reasonable and unreasonable, didn't succeed in locating the whereabouts of the young girl. And so days and nights went by, and as happens in every small village inhabited by simple folk, the favorite subject of conversation became that ill-omened night and its ghastly events. The result of this was that every villager would, with the setting of the sun, take to the safety of his house.

"On one of those long winter nights dreadful screams were heard, screams that brought terror to all who heard them. People at the time knew the source of these screams but no one had the courage to go out and satisfy their curiosity about them, fear confining everyone to the darkness of their homes. When the sun's rays stretched out, bringing light to the world of that poor expanse of land called a village, all the people were in turmoil. As though in prior agreement, they all set off for that house. When they arrived at the courtyard of the house they found someone's form hidden away in a corner, all curled up, its head almost buried in the sand.

"The eldest of them went forward and touched the body's shoulder, at which a scream of terror emanated from the crouching form, after which it went into a faint. None of them knew who this person was. He had a look of neglect, for he had youthful features despite the pallor, and was . . . ?

"They carried him to the house of the eldest of them and for several hours they sat around and stared. When he began to regain consciousness and to be aware that there were people around him and that he wasn't in another world, he told them a story that froze the blood in their veins. Being a stranger to the district, he had found, on arriving at night, nowhere to lay his head other than the courtyard of that murky place. As he had readied himself to go to sleep, he had heard mumbling behind him. Turning around he had seen a young girl of ravishing appearance wholly out of place with the alleyways of that filthy quarter. The girl was clad in what looked like an aba that was draped across her head and reached down to her feet. When the girl motioned to him to follow her into the house, he did so without uttering a word, as he was too exhausted to reply. The black curtains were drawn and the place gave out a musty, unclean odor, and there was a small lamp there that scarcely provided gave off any light. At this, the man noticed something odd about the girl which he could not define, for her features were rigid, her eyes seemingly petrified, and her long nails repellent. He had shuddering sensations of terror at the situation he was in. He tried to draw back but her eyes seemed to nail him to the spot. Her aba fell from her head and he saw that it was shaven, its veins bulging. Suddenly she broke into laughter, which grew louder and more hysterical. Stepping back, he tried to find the door. He moved off, then tried to run, using all his strength combined with a will to survive. In fact, he did not move from where he stood as though he were running on a treadmill. And then, quite suddenly, he found himself falling into space. He felt pairs of hands hurling him back and forth, after which they dragged him outside and cast him into that remote corner. He began screaming until there was no strength left inside him to make any sound. And so he had remained motionless until he sensed someone, the following morning, touching his shoulder.

"This incredible story began to invade every house, every mind and, every heart, until people were too scared even to pass by a road at whose farthest end lay this house. Whenever some tragedy or disaster struck the village, the blame would be laid at the door of the house. It was thus that a few of the villagers, those who were easily influenced, decided to leave the village for fear that some disaster would befall them on account of that accursed house—or so they believed.

"As everything in life is born small and then grows larger, except, that is, for sorrow and anxiety, which grow smaller with the passage of time, so this story died down until it was brought back to life by some chance occurence in the village, though things would calm down once again, while remaining nonetheless susceptible to the slightest of winds to set it ablaze once more.

"Days, months, and years passed, and he who had heard the story as a child would recount it when he had grown old, and each narrator would add some fresh terrors of his own. Thus the story was not the property of any one person.

"What had happened would have passed into legend had it not been for the fact that also on a wintry night some time after that former winter, whisperings began to spread about the existence of a ghost in the shape of an old woman who went roaming around between the houses in the quarter. No one ventured to either confirm or deny these rumors, and no one was able to ascertain their origin, though they spread like fire through straw, for bad and mysterious news always finds people ready to take it in. Once again the locals kept to their houses at sunset, emerging only when the sun was set firmly in the center of the sky.

"We know that in every place and time where there is someone timid, there is also someone adventurous. And so it was that some of the young men in the village decided to solve the mystery of the story related by the old man. In groups of two they hid themselves at the head of the dusty narrow lanes that connected the village houses. They agreed to call out if they saw anything strange or suspicious. They spent their first night like this, also the second and the third, with nothing happening until boredom overtook them. Then, suddenly, on the fourth night, two of the men, having taken up their position on one of the roads leading to the house on the hillside, saw a light moving along the road, one that swung right to left. The two men stood rooted to the spot, unable to move or call out to their companions. What they saw was an old woman carrying an ancient lamp and treading along heavily. As she drew close to the two men, she suddenly turned off into one of the narrow alleyways and disappeared from view, and they were unable to catch up with her. Despite the pervading darkness, save for the faint light from the lamp, they had nevertheless been able to make out her wrinkled features and to ascertain that she was not one of the old women of the village. She too saw them and then disappeared from view. The two young men left their place before dawn and went to find their companions. They related what had happened and apologized for not calling out to the others, having been unable to do so.

"The group repeated their attempts to discover the mystery of that old woman, but she didn't appear again, though stories confirmed that the lamplight was seen from time to time inside that deserted house on the hill."

The old man ended his story by saying, "I was one of those young men who hid themselves at the top of those lanes, and to this day we still take turns to watch over those roads but to no avail, for the old woman hasn't appeared again, and we never came to know the secret of her story or to find an explanation for the events that occurred in that house. But, in the minds of all the locals, the place still bears a curse."

Fishhooks

Nasser Jubran

A s usual they went out that day in the afternoon carrying their fishing gear and some provisions of food and water. They were going out to sea in their large boat whose prow rose up like a legendary bird, while behind them gleamed a storm of foam, sprayed in all directions, making of the disturbed waves the delta of an exhausted river.

They set off, with the sea a vast expanse, leaving behind them the empty concrete cities and a ribbon of widely spaced date palms standing erect above the shoreline like women anxiously awaiting the return of their breadwinners.

The land grew slowly dimmer and dimmer until there was nothing left but water.

Disarrayed clouds bringing the odor of saltpeter quickly flitted by. The sun cast its slanting firebrand in a slow rolling motion, washing the ocean with its ruptured rays in a silvery flash of light that clouded the vision.

Singing birds swirled in an open space, repeating their enchanting dance of soaring into the air and then diving down to snatch up small fishes.

Suddenly Jassem called out, pointing ahead, "There . . . over there." The boat sped on, with Khamees handling the rudder.

"Come along, throw out your lines, fellows," Rasheed called out to them.

They let out their lines, with their hooks empty of any bait.

The boat combed the sea, coming and going, rushing off at full speed with the lines rising to the surface as hands grabbed at them whenever a fish was hooked.

Said called out joyfully as he drew in his line, "However devilish the weather, you can always catch something."

Hamad, too, drew in his line, laughing at his comrade Said's words.

The speeding boat left behind a trail of foam. Salem al-Heer, too, drew in his line, detached the fish, and threw out the line again. Moments later he had to reel it in again.

Everyone was busy catching fish. An hour went by, then another, with the Gulf giving up its bounty. They changed their position, moving north and following those swarms of birds that were enamored of water. They were enjoying a tremendous feeling of elation. Their lines were like the strings of a musical instrument whose reverberations were those of the sea and of man, while the sun was an orange of live coals that moved down into an empty chasm.

"Stop the engine," Salem called out. "It seems all our lines have got into a large fish."

The engine came to a stop and the boat was left to drift without anchor, jostled by small waves. Everyone was bewildered in the face of the unknown, enveloped in an awesome silence. Hands gently drew in the lines as though in dread at their being swallowed and taken into the stomach of a large fish. One line after another was snapped loose. Bodies moved closer to one another and between them took hold of the weight with an overwhelming sense of expectation, worry, and caution. There was complete silence: something heavy that gave out no movement or resistance. At that moment they were all convinced that there was no fish there. Cautiously they drew in the lines. Something indistinct was floating there, its features disappearing into shades of red as the sun scalded the horizon. They could not make out what it was, but when it came nearer they were stunned, their bodies trembled, and they began stammering among themselves as they made out a floating, bloated human corpse. It was shielded by a military uniform, the buttons of which were missing. Through the tatters of clothes could be made out the lines of a disfigured face with a shaven head. The smell from the body mingled with that of the sea. They stared hard at it, searching deep into their memories, but when they failed to identify it they decided to search the pockets, but they found no personal information or document to give them a clue as to whose body it was. As they did this they wondered about what to do with the body: to take it on board or to let it continue floating about in the waters of the Gulf? A boat from the naval fleet that had imposed its authority over the Gulf drew close, obscuring the beauty of the horizon. Fishes leaped about in alarm at the sudden intrusion that had disturbed the silence and beauty of the place. The corpse had moved far off, and the boat swayed out of control like a small wooden plank being jostled by waves that were dispatching it to faraway shores.

They ceased to be concerned with either the floating corpse or the naval fleet. Their whole attention was centered on the boat and rescuing it from sinking. Scattered misty clouds carried off the smell of saltpeter and of a sprawling corpse floating on the waters of the sea, as it moved off slowly and disappeared into the waiting darkness.

Grief of the Night Bird

Ibrahim Mubarak

A path extending to very great distances, a time whose twists and turns cannot be counted. Pictures that never conform. Hamdan is united with his old life, is in harmony with it, while Said is a child now facing a new passage. He is learning from Hamdan how to call to hawks.

"It's very simple," he told Said. "A little practice and you'll be able to make the hawk's decoy."

The detached wings of a bird or a pigeon are tied together to make the shape of a live bird, then it is waved about in the air. When the hawk sees it, it speeds off, like one hungry for its prey, and when it takes a grip on the wings, it is drawn away, and then it is given its evening meal of meat or pigeon. After repeating the exercise every evening for several months, the hawk or falcon becomes tame with its master.

Hamdan laughed heartily at this summary and simplification of the special characteristics and life of the hawk.

"My dear young chap," he said, "if it was all that simple anyone at all could become a falconer or someone able to catch hawks. It's a big subject and a lot more complicated.

"No one understands about hawks other than those who know the desert and its peculiarities, the methods of hunting, the game animals and the narrow mountain passes—only the strong and intelligent men of the desert, the trainers of these beautiful birds of prey."

Hamdan is from old times, a falconer who has had experience of life when it was extremely barren and poverty-stricken in every way, when there was nothing except what nature had bestowed in the way of hunting on land and sea. And to be in balance with life and defeat its barrenness, he would adapt his equipment to each time of year.

In the winter he depended on hunting with hawks, in addition to what he owned in the way of goats and camels, while in the summer he moved close to the shore and the sea, relying on the life of the seashore by fishing and benefiting from the produce of the date palms.

In this period he would take care of his hawks, doing everything possible to see that the birds renewed their feathers in preparation for winter when he began a special summer program known as 'seasoning.' Because the seashore is extremely hot and in times of drought all the birds migrate and there is no meat available in the fishermen's village, he set traps for cats which he then slaughtered to give their meat to the hawks.

Some people disapproved of this dubious practice, but Hamdan would justify it by saying that his birds were quickly changing their feathers and thus the program of 'seasoning' them had succeeded and he would soon be able to get them ready for wintertime.

Young Said was astounded at the way the falcon would hurl itself off at amazing speed. When it attacked the decoy or the pigeon that Hamdan threw to the bird every evening, he made a point of attending this demonstration before each sunset, the time for Hamdan to call to his hawks.

A long time ago this good fine man traveled away, and the life of the seacoast and the desert changed, but nothing remained in the mind of Said except for his great love for hawks and hawking.

The city had grown larger and had changed in every way, had in fact become one of the civilized cities, bearing the contradictory characteristics of large cities in every way: in the absurd and the beautiful, and in its clamor and strange and extraordinary ways, where the new and the old merged, and where strangers, with their different customs, had multiplied, while it was in a state between opening out, disintegrating, conserving, and taking root.

Said himself had become like that, for he was contradictory by nature, and held different views and opinions, not knowing a single path to journey along, for things had been discarded from his life and new things added, as he stayed clinging to some of the old alongside the newest crazes of the age. He had got to know new fashions that had come to the city, and had adopted them in accordance with what was new in life, in addition to the past of the desert and the sea. He loved hawks and hawking, but he also loved the city and its hubbub and its new ways. Thus in the winter he roamed the deserts to hunt game animals, while in the summer he was a frequenter of cafés and nightclubs, and saw nothing wrong with that.

He lived life and faced it with the old and the new. What does it mean that man is in accord with his surroundings and at peace with himself, unconcerned by the criticism of others, living solely for the day?

He always said, "Greetings to the new life, it is a time that deserves to be valued and it should be given the opportunity for its style to be understood. There is no need for everything in the distant past to be ever-present.

"By itself the falcon is the most beautiful thing in my life, and having loved it since I was young and had my first peep at life, I gave to it eternal adoration, so there's nothing surprising in the fact that this love goes on being a part of me.

"It's my constant companion and is ever with me. This beloved companion must remain constantly with me in any situation I find myself in, for it is the dearest friend in this life."

It is a stiflingly hot evening with very high humidity and not a whiff of air.

"Nothing will quench this thirst except a really cold bottle of something and some highly efficient air-conditioning."

He stopped his car in the hotel's packed car park.

Carrying his hawk, he proceeded slowly toward the entrance. Steam on the glass made it impossible to see through. He pushed open the glass door and walked toward the bar, crossing the big lounge.

He attracted attention, especially from the foreigners, but he paid attention to no one for he knew his way to his favorite corner. The waitress attended to him with a broad smile, then brought him his usual order.

He caressed the hawk, stroking it on the head and wings, then made firm the threads of the beautifully embellished hood that he had recently bought.

He put the hawk beside him on the edge of the wooden bar and let his imagination wander with the blaring of the changing music and the colored lights that surrounded the place.

He observed people coming in and out, and those who were intoxicated and dancing to the music.

The place had filled up with smoke, and the noise of hookahs being smoked could be heard as a fervor pervaded everyone with nightfall. And as the evening wore on, different groups of customers joined in.

Among them was a man wearing local dress. He was smartly turned out and walked along haughtily, while behind him was a woman wearing a black aba, clasped in tightly at the waist, her face covered by a black veil.

She was tall like a bamboo shoot, while the man was broad-shouldered and squarely built.

The man walked to a far corner with low lighting. The waiter brought them both hookahs, a bottle of drink, and two glasses.

They both joined the others in increasing the amount of smoke. The place changed into a dance floor with dancing, singing, and smoke, mixed with the sounds of voices and whisperings in the corners.

Some people lost all sense of dignity, breaking all barriers of decency. The corner into which the man and the woman had sneaked was pervaded by an unusual commotion.

Having taken off the aba and the veil, she had then walked into the middle of the dance floor and had begun dancing like a professional, while the man was trying to stop her by dragging her back into his corner. As voices were raised in shouts, the guard at the bar and some of the men working there tried to intervene, but the woman was in such a state that there was no smoothing over the quarrel.

"I hate you," she told the man furiously. "Our time together is over, everything between us is finished! Look at what time it is: from now on I'm free to do as I please."

She rushed back to the corner and took up the aba and the veil in one hand and her handbag in the other.

Under the lights her bare legs appeared as beautiful as gold, while her breasts, seeking to make their escape from the loosened dress, looked like sparkles of silver. Having let her golden hair fall down her back, she proceeded like a spear, gloriously elegant, toward the door. Before going through it, she gave the man a challenging glance.

He followed her out in disarray, muttering incomprehensibly.

People were taken up with the noise and the music and the whisperings about the scene they had just witnessed. Said, too, was curious about what had gone on at the bar and he moved away from the hawk to discover what was going on.

A drunk foreigner came up to the hawk and protested about it being tied with cords and its being bound to the stand, and for having the hood placed over its head. Without Said noticing, the man undid the cords and took away the hood.

He had no sooner done so than the hawk flew off round the room, banging against people's heads as it tried to get out of this large cage filled with smoke, noise, and bright lights.

Women screamed in terror and everyone tried to escape. The music stopped as the musicians took flight, even barmen fled in fear from this angry predatory bird that was circling around from corner to corner.

Only Said ran after his hawk, trying to calm it down. The whole place was by now empty, all except for the vacant chairs, silent glasses, and Said and his hawk.

The hawk came to rest in one corner and Said in another. He cursed this hateful day and his stupid behavior.

"My dear hawk," he told it. "I apologize to you. I am ashamed of myself and the way I have behaved. I promise you that I'll never come back to this place.

"O beautiful one, everyone has fled and only you and I are left. Come, let's get away from the smoke and the noise and the sickness. Beloved one, nothing is worthy of you but the clear sky and the clean desert."

A long time of quiet silence ruled during which Said kept on repeating the name of his hawk which responded by moving its head up and down, an indication which Said knew informed him that his hawk had understood his call.

Going up to it, he fixed the cords attaching it to the stand, then put it on his right hand. As he raised it, the bird gently flapped its wings. Then he placed the hood over its head.

The hawk calmed down, and he stroked its head, back, and chest. "One day they'll all run away," he told it. "You alone never will."

He walked outside, joyful at being in possession of his hawk.

The Old Woman
Maryam Al Saedi

Her children and everyone else call her "the old woman." She's an old lady from times back. Her clothes have the smell of her sheep and that rusty smell of the ancient trunk in which she keeps her things. She could never understand why she had to be 'appropriately dressed,' for she never thought that she wasn't. In fact, she'd never once paid attention to what she looked like. She was one of those women who had had a lot of children without allowing their husbands to see their faces, the face being—as she believed—a shameful part of the body. Those same women didn't call their husbands by their names but solely by the words "the man," for this is what they were. She was one of those women who had lived without it occurring to them for an instant that they themselves could be something other than the wives of So-and-so and the mothers of So-and-so or the owners of the sheep having such-and-such a brand. She had got used to the faraway life of the Bedouin: desert, sands, and thirst for as far as the eye could see. The young children would be in the tent and before nightfall one would have to finish milking the ewes. A crust of bread all mixed up with the ashes of the fire would be the most delicious meal after a day of never-ending heat and hardship. No, there was no hardship. No, it was just a day. There was nothing never-ending. No, it was just a day.

She knew only that days had to be like that. Her ewes were her
daughters and her rams were her sons. She knew them by their
names, their colors, their shapes. They were more precious than
her own sons. In those days she was "the woman" and was not
known by any name. Her children only became aware of her
name when they had to obtain a death certificate. Her relationship
with the husband was something understood and accepted. Many
were the quarrels she had with him because of her sheep and his
sheep, but in the end he was the man, and in the end she was the
woman. It was something understood and accepted.

◆

When the small children grew up she came to be known as "the
old woman." "The old man" had died ages ago, so there was
nothing for it but for her to ask to be accommodated in the house
of one of the sons. The sons had got older, had really grown up,
and it had become beyond the capability of the old woman to be
acquainted with them.

The eldest son was now a high-ranking officer in the army.
The second had an even greater rank in the police, and the
next in line was a highly regarded employee in a governmental
organization, while the one after him was a university professor,
and the youngest had gone abroad to study and hadn't yet
returned. The daughters, too, had their important roles. The old
woman would refuse to leave her tent. People would reproach
the sons for neglecting their old mother, and they would lose
something of their self-respect each time she was mentioned,
and they wouldn't know how to free themselves from the offense
committed against the old woman and their own shame.

They would insist that she come to live with them, and
would tempt her with the cold water they could provide her

with, the air-conditioned rooms and the soft bed, with the sons who would make up to her the years of privation, the grandsons who would take care of her, and they would promise to take her to visit her sheep every week, and eventually she would give in to their entreaties.

◆

In the older son's house she found the room cold, the bedding cold, and the house cold. She forgot that she had a voice, for she no longer had any sheep to talk to. As for the grandchildren, she didn't know what they looked like because they were at school and hadn't yet come back. She thought the maid was the son's wife and was amazed at how she didn't understand Arabic.

When it became very cold she wanted to move to another son's house, then to another's and yet another's. Then to a daughter's, and to another daughter's and to another's. She moved between them all and found all their houses too cold and wanted to return to her sheep, but one after the other they had all died, and she no longer saw them every week, or every month, or even every year. One of the old women told her, during a brief visit, that all her sheep had died. Of course she didn't believe her and accused her of having stolen them and wanted to check this for herself. She went out into the street wanting to return to the tent, to her beloved sheep, for the red ewe had been about to give birth and she wanted to know whether it had produced a ewe or a ram—or perhaps twins. Did it give birth to red ones or to black, or would she find them white-colored? Perhaps some of this and some of that. She had to see them, because young sheep could come to harm in one way or another, and grown-up sheep needed looking after, and she'd been away for a long time. She saw nothing, she must go back. Wanting to go back to her sheep, she put on her thin, faded aba. In the middle of the crowded street her daughter's neighbor recognized her and took her back to her daughter's house. "She was standing in the middle of the street like a feather in a storm." The neighbor's boys were laughing together. "She was like a witch on a broomstick—she was a frightening sight." Looking at her patched dress and threadbare aba, her son's religious wife said, "I ask forgiveness of God, your mother's flesh can all be seen—an old woman with no sense of shame." They all had the same opinion of her and expressed it in the phrase: "You've disgraced us among people, you old woman—may God guide you aright." The old woman went back to her cold room at the back of the family house. Her son's wife brought her some new clothes, her son brought her new shoes, her daughter brought her new abas and shawls, and her son's other wife brought her perfumes and new veils. They ordered the servant to prepare her hot food, to wash her bedding and fumigate her room. They bought her pure honey to drink and chose a special maid to serve her and keep an eye on her. The old woman threw out all the new things into the nearby garbage bin. She got back her patched dress and her worn out shoes and set about stitching them up, and she put her aba into her old box full of the smell of rust, sheep, old age, and of the ancient tent.

◆

People saw that the grown-up sons had not been neglectful of the old woman. But the old woman herself was difficult, and when people realized this the consciences of the sons relaxed. The old woman kept to her room, never leaving it, and no one disturbed her seclusion except for the maid who would bring her plates of food that she prepared each time in the same way, for the old woman wouldn't eat their food. "The old woman's a disaster—may God give the children patience with her," thought the maid.

"What does the old woman eat?" it occurred to the son to ask of the maid in a moment of revelation at lunchtime. "She eats yogurt and bread that she keeps in that box of hers." The son shakes his head in astonishment and eats his lunch, while the wife mutters a silent prayer that when she grows old God may not make her into a difficult old woman who torments her children and shames them in front of people.

The maid began refusing to sleep in the same room as the old woman, for she would talk to herself all the time. Even in her sleep she would say all sorts of things, calling out to her sheep, quarrelling with her husband, and calling out to small children to come back to the tent before darkness came.

❖

The old woman died. Everything had been made ready for this event, with large tents set up for the ceremony of mourning. A mass of people attended: the friends of the children who all held high positions, their neighbors and their colleagues at work, women neighbors and friends and the women friends of the granddaughters, and the friends of the grandsons who had at last come back from school. Even the son who had gone abroad returned to receive, in company with his brothers, those presenting their condolences. "We wouldn't be able to look people in the face if he didn't return for his mother's ceremony of mourning." Everything went off just as it should. Everyone was able to look people in the face and the old woman was laid to rest in the ground with due propriety.

Ripe Dates and Date Palms
Hareb al-Dhaheri

The child's body was frail, and his tight, ragged clothes were badly torn and full of holes, the ends dirty and giving out a stench of sweat, the product of weary steps running through places he had traversed, while others still awaited his beaming face.

Stinging words, as searing as the flame of the sun's rays, were thrust at him by his mother. "Go at once like lightning and bring the basket of ripe dates from among the date palms. Off with you and don't waste time standing around in the streets like the stuffed skin of a young camel."

In his throat was the bitterness of morning. He turned off into the twisting pathways between the houses. Open-mouthed amidst a mass of flies, he went like the wind itself, the end of his dishdasha shoved into his mouth as he bit on it so that it wouldn't impede him. He knew that if he was late his mother would scold him throughout the day or that he would be punished.

When he came to the date palms, they looked so tall, and between the gaps trees cowered, garbed in the greenness of thick grass. His feet disappeared into unseen patches where he was stung by thorns.

His face looked damp. The moistness of his hair and fuzzy sweat attached themselves to scraps of dust. His body disappeared from sight, and no sound of his footsteps could be heard. He appeared amid the grass as a disheveled head, with two staring bloodshot eyes that gleamed in idiotic perplexity through thickets of fear.

The trunks of date palms met as though they were corpses mangled by the ants that had penetrated their leaves, while scraps of ripe dates, strewn about beneath them, gave out a fermented smell mixed with that of the date palms and the water-sodden roots. The hand of the man in charge had not, it seemed, troubled about the date palms. The extensive remains of garbage, beneath which legends muttered, entangled an unknown world that embraced the innocence of a face, hateful fear, and enchanting words.

He had been with his father on the day when he had told him about some heads that had been buried here. They were war dead. When he had asked his father about their bodies, he had been overcome by an uneasy silence. He looked as though he were without a throbbing heart and the blood had compressed itself into his face.

His mother's voice still pealed fear into him. Two eyes danced with hollow phantoms interweaving in awesome nooks, while the sounds of predatory birds could be heard from the tree tops. A shredded distortion, the remains of the bones over the eyes and the stumps of the limbs of a white man crucified on the date palms.

The date palms seemed to lie in wait for him as he searched for the overseer who, it seems, had not been looking after them for some time so that they looked soulless. They had dried up, their fruit scattered by the winds.

He was still leaning against the whisperings of his loneliness; and, as a result of his fear, he made up his mind to leave. But his mother's words, which she had driven into him so deeply took hold of him once more, so he appeared to be taking his time, waiting for the overseer rather than for his mother's punishment. She had pelted him with sharp words: a whole stick would be broken on his back if he didn't come back with the basket of ripe dates. The words she had flung at him had made it clear that he would find the basket under the trunks of the palm-trees that had been thrown down—just as the overseer had told her.

What would happen if he were not to trouble about it and did not go back? He would remain confined under the concentration of shade, a source of noise forever recalcitrant. Cats meowed loudly, following in his tracks, entwining themselves around his feet as though playing a game; to hide their pain, they pretended to be oblivious of him, concealing themselves among the trees before returning angrily to make their presence felt. They were dying of starvation: the overseer had not fed them, all of which suggested that he hadn't embraced the date palms and climbed up them. He hadn't come since several mornings ago, when he had opened the arteries of the watercourses so that the water might sparkle limpidly, penetrating the trees' limbs and opening their appetites to life.

As forenoon arrived he tied around his waist the special rope used for climbing up date palms. The date palm clasped him to its breast, as a loving mother would her child. He reached the top of its throne, intoxicated, hurried on by the solitude of the fresh air. With infinite care he inserted his hand between the thorns to gather up the dates tremblingly, filling the basket and began to make his descent, the date palm, bearing him on its waist, right until he touched ground.

He made his way to the date palm sloping against the mud wall and gathered up the Kheneizi and Bumaan dates, also from the other date palms, so as to fill the basket. Normally he put the basket in its usual place under the trunk of the date palm that had been collapsing for some time. Now, though, his steps took him to the nearby date palms. It was as though he had emerged from a cave to throw his body into the watercourse to take a wash with the overseers, his companions in the job.

They were taking a short break when they were surprised by the child with his thin body and face swollen from stings whose cause was unknown. He saw them about to put on their tattered clothes.

The overseer gave him a basket of dates and said to him, "Give my greetings to your family"—dates that he had just gathered up with his own hand.

When, at first glance, the mother saw the dates, she let out a moan, while a shout grew within her. "Where are the dates?" she asked. "This basket is too small and won't be enough for your grandfather, nor for your auntie's house—and what about us? There won't be enough for lunch. The best dates have been taken by the overseer to the market and he's given us an empty basket."

The Little Tree | *Nasser al-Dhaheri*

Someone older than me informed me that a man once came holding the seedling of a lotus tree that he had planted alongside the mud house near the date palms and that he had then gone away.

People said, "What's this dry seedling?" Others made a diminutive of the word and said, "What's this tiny seedling?"

Young girls got married and their husbands continued to work in the Trucial Oman Scouts. They became pregnant and gave birth to boys and girls who began mouthing words, walking and playing beneath the shade of the little tree.

The women, when they went off to fill their water jars, would say, "The tiny seedling has grown," while the men, when changing detachments and regiments and were finally settled, would say, "By God, how the little tree has grown!"

The big lotus tree that lives in the old Nahayani school found itself a companion that grew bigger every day, and the old women who resorted to the old Kindi Hospital would sit around under it, displaying their wares—veils, perfumes, and folk medicines—and filling the place with stories and ceaseless chatter. The children and the dawn were part of the night's darkness. They would get to their feet to pick the lotus fruit of the little tree, filling the pockets of their school uniforms. The little tree was a foster mother for the she-donkey of Khamees bin Jumaa, and the girls' swings hung down from its branches. The little tree had become a great tree under which people sought shade; it also provided shade for the large army lorries, and for people crossing with their caravans of camels. Its open space, screened off from the burning eye of the sun, was a playground for children, a place for animals to be slaughtered when there were guests, for cooking pots at weddings, and from its branches were fashioned the sticks that were the delight of the religious prefect.

Rain poured down, becoming a torrent, riverbeds were formed, while the tree remained put. Every year it would bear fruit even though the taste wasn't up to that of the Zakhmi lotus tree, but yet it did give fruit and continued to do so, its branches tenderly stretching out over the mud houses that had begun to show their age. Everyone, young and old, would say, "I remember the seedling from the time I began to walk"—but they didn't tell you how old it was.

Suddenly, house by house, everyone took off. Some came to rest in al-Mutamid, some in Oud at-Toba, yet others in Kuwaitat, and the people of the coast who used to come every summer no longer did so. The little tree remained on its own, except for the occasional stranger who would come to it from time to time, delighting in an intoxicating afternoon nap, or a camel would savor its leaves, which had begun to dry up, while the old women who used to display their goods underneath it now showed a fondness for air-conditioning or were separated from the tree by roads and bridges, which required cars that made them dizzy to get to it. The caravans of camels that used to enjoy its shade were long gone, while the quarter's destitute now amused themselves with their cars and mobile phones, and with summer and winter journeys.

The tree remained on its own, now merely the remnant of a large, decrepit tree, while the neighboring date palms had scarcely begun to stick their heads above the cement walls. The open space, verdant with the vital movement of people, had now become a wasteland, all except for a municipality truck whose driver stole some of his working hours by lying prone underneath it, and the alleyway that was once traversed by the feet of men, women, and children has now become like a bald pate. The tree has remained on its own, its green tresses having fallen out, its lotus fruit having dried up in its mothering branches, and the faces that used daily to look after it are no longer alive. It is all alone and its own death is on the way.

The Peddler

Muhsin Soleiman

I still remember him well as he carried a great bundle on his back. He would make the rounds of the lanes and alleys, calling out in his loud voice, "Things for sale . . . things . . . ." The servants would hear him and hurry off to my mother. "Mama, Masood him at the door," and my mother would leave what she was doing and rush off to him. Generally my mother at this time would be pounding the pestle, washing the rice, or cutting up the onions. I would assume that on this day she was chopping onions and would wash her face and eyes well after doing so. She would put on her veil or lower her wrapper over her face. Masood would let fall the bundle outside in front of the door and spread it out to set off the traditional things he had, such as perfumes, pieces of cloth, watches, and odds and ends. He would sit down, squatting on his heels and glance to his right and left. If a woman passed by the house he would attract her attention by calling out, "Come, come, all velly cheap . . . all no price." The place would fill up with clients, householders and their children, a scene I would find repeated weekly in front of every house in the quarter.

Yes, I still remember him well. He was Masood, an Afghan man with an oval face under his large turban, and a body with muscular arms. His dense beard stretched from his temples halfway down his chest. God had bestowed on him a snowy whiteness of complexion and an enviable determination. Masood bested his competitors in the business and became one of the prominent personalities in the old districts of Sharjah—Sharq and Majarra and the neighboring ones. Even after the development of the place and our move to a new area, Masood himself developed and moved around as a hawker amongst us.

I watch my mother as she argues with him and am amazed at her strong personality. She is bargaining with him and persuading him to lower his prices by more than half. And I still remember, when I saw a toy that pleased me, how my mother succeeded in taking off the naught from the 150 dirhams. I was also amazed at him as a person: he was as patient as a camel, towering aloft like a date palm, yet he was always the one defeated in a bargaining deal. I would stand leaning against him, with my hand on his thigh while he was buying and selling and exchanging old for new without growing weary or bored, and I would ask myself: How much does he buy his goods for and what percentage of profit does he make, if any at all? He would jabber away in the sort of Arabic spoken by Afghans, and when I talked to him I was forced to lift my head up high as though addressing the sky. He would joke with me and stroke my head, though he wouldn't stop scolding me. My friends and I would often annoy him with phrases such as "Get on with you, you donkey," mispronouncing the words in the way he did. Sometimes I would see in his eyes a pressing need to make a sale when he would sell at any price, and many a time—I don't know why—I would be beset with doubts about him.

When he was older and his beard had become red in color, and he had been away for several months, I saw him branching off from the main street in our direction. He was driving a green-colored Datsun with a number plate consisting of four figures: in appearance and smell it greatly resembled the taxis of today. He took me with him in his car. I was struck by it; everything in it shook and moved. He told me to hang on tight to my seat and I felt as though I were riding a horse.

Masood became an inseparable part of our popular heritage, despite what anyone might say; along with the water carrier and the sorcerer he took his place in the depths of society, promoting his new goods, vaunting the GAT Agreement and free trade, spreading wide open his bundle of goods, calling out in his loud voice about his wares and pieces of cloth.

After the country's economic upturn, Masood disappeared and went away for about five years. He was the subject of conversation for the morning sessions of the mothers of the quarter. There were all sorts of contradictory stories about him. There were those who said that he had gone into partnership with one of the well-known investors, and, having made his coup, had then fled the country. Our neighbor Umm Hammoud swore by all that was sacred that she saw him at the Dubai Festival with his beard shaved off and that he was selling expensive brands of tobacco. As for the most likely story, it was said that he had traveled to his country to take part in a holy war.

Our Indian neighbor brought along a copy of *The Gulf News*, which showed a picture of the provisional head of state Karzai, with Masood sitting right behind him, his hands joined together like a genie from a lamp. Later we sat in front of the television awaiting the news of the provisional government, all of us expecting to see Masood on Aljazeera or Abu Dhabi television, when we saw him in the middle of the screen in the shape of an officer, and on another station as a barber and shoemaker. His eyes looked like those of Tony Blair and his nose exactly like that of Bush. Today we heard the following urgent item of news: "Masood has vanished in mysterious circumstances among the ravines of Tora Bora and the search for him is still ongoing. . . ."

The Sound
of Singing | *Salma Matar Seif*

I 'll cut your throat, you animal," said my grandfather, "if I
see you again with that awful woman."
He was pressing down on my neck with his hulking foot. The
harsher his threats against me the more his foot embedded itself in
my flesh. Then he moved away, leaving my body like some great
throbbing heart. I felt that I was being expanded and contracted,
like some desert plant ablaze under the scorching sun.

I approached my heavily breathing mother and looked into
her eyes and face. "Does he stop me from seeing her because
she's black?"

"Your grandfather, my girl, hates everyone who disobeys
him," said my mother. "He has the heart of a pearling ship's
captain who coldly buries his divers in the sea's depths. I really
doubt his ability to feel the pain you suffer as you lie under his
foot. Don't provoke the fury he has for the woman."

I wondered why he prevented me from seeing Dahma, for I
had noticed that his state changed as soon as he came to hear
that Dahma was living in our vicinity. I found him most of the
time grave-faced, staring ahead of him, and eating frugally. Only
occasionally would he leave the house. I would see him lying
on his side with a glum expression inhabiting the cruel features
of his face. At dawn—I had the habit of getting up several

times during the night—the sound of his coughing would reach me, together with the smell of the tobacco he smoked in his narghile. I was convinced that something was so upsetting my grandfather that it was making him pallid and ill. This change had come about with the arrival of the woman in our quarter. And when he learned I had visited Dahma, he fell into a rage, exploding in my mother's face and throwing me to the ground and beating me with a severity not used against someone of one's own blood.

I continued paying visits to Dahma, drawn there by my grandfather's hatred for the woman. I was overcome by surprise, for I had seen nothing bad in her to cause me to fear her. In fact, the woman was so beautiful that one was afraid to stare at her for any length of time. She had a physique that was formidable, like that of some mythical goddess, captivating in the way that a fine woman captivates a repressed mortal. The palm of her hand was surprisingly broad, while her head had the roundness of a pigeon's, with facial features that seemed chiseled out of rock.

When I drew close to her I saw her brown neck twisted by cruel blows, as though she had been whipped mercilessly. During my encounter with her, she did not come out of her silence, conversing merely through a wide smile, which she feebly gave from time to time, while I followed her wild look, and I yearned for her to utter. I left her place with a thirst for Dahma, this woman who was tearing my grandfather apart.

"Mother, what's the woman's story?"

My mother, too, was unhappy with me asking about Dahma and fled from my questioning like someone running away from a blazing fire.

"Mother, I shall go to Dahma and my grandfather can do what he likes about it."

My mother took hold of my hand and I sat down beside her. Her body was shaking as though with a fever. "This woman has a bad reputation, and . . . ."

I went to Dahma. There was an opaqueness about her eyes like cumulus clouds moving in the sky without sending down any rain. I examined her face, her hands, her bosom, and the rest of her body. I did not see it as a body that could lie back and indulge in fornication. I was seeing her in her mythical form, erect like a tree that seeds itself. I feel that my mother's eyes avoid the truth.

"Mother, what's the woman's story?"

My mother's face was afire with cruel yellowness. Swallowing her spittle, she begged me urgently. "Your grandfather will not spare you. Keep away from the woman."

"Mother, I'm going to ask my grandfather about her."

My mother made a moaning noise as she lowered her eyes to the ground. "The woman you're interested in is nothing but an immoral drunk. Look at her eyes."

At dawn, my fear of my grandfather's authority did not check my impulse and I hurried off breathlessly to the woman. I sought asylum with her, my gaze directed at her confused and deranged eyes. I saw the signs of which my mother had spoken: red veins filling the inside of her eye-sockets.

"Grandpa, why do you stop me from seeing Dahma? Is it because she's black? She's beautiful—I've begun to be in love with her."

My grandfather took hold of my hair with both hands, hurting my scalp: it was his sole means of dealing with me.

"You're a disobedient little devil, and I'll break this head of yours. You ask about this whore. Ask, too, about her ten bastard sons."

I waited for the time when my grandfather went out to the gathering of men in the middle of the village souk, and I hurried off to the woman. I don't know the secret of why I lost my mental balance over this woman. My grandfather says she has ten bastard sons. Yet she is a woman on her own, sunk in silence, and around her hovers a secret. It is because of this secret that he beats me cruelly and exposes me to his filthy smell when he is in a rage. And what astonishes me is that my grandfather goes all weak at the mere mention of that woman.

When I went to her I found she was not alone. Beside her was an aged poet whom I know well and see walking along the roads and alleyways, and whose voice I sometimes hear at dawn fervently declaiming. He was sitting beside her, relaxed and happy. I told myself: perhaps this madman is the woman's secret, so I'll ask him. She drew me close to her and I breathed in the smell that emanated from her, like the smell of a date-palm. When I scrutinized her closely, she was not in a position for me to talk to her or to ask the poet for his view. I was tongue-tied and uttered not a word. The poet, too, added nothing. She passed her hand over my chest without making any conversation.

I circled around my mother. With tears I pleaded with her to tell me something about Dahma. She freed herself from me and made off to my grandfather, but he was not there. "She's a crazy woman with no one to tell her how to behave. Her mother was utterly insane and would go out into the highways naked and enter people's houses and refuse to put anything on to cover herself. The people here used to throw stones at her and beat her." At this, my mother stared into my eyes and said, "Then she was found murdered on a rubbish dump." My mother fell silent and I saw in her face a furrow of fear. She turned to me with the look of a wounded animal.

"Why did her mother go mad?"

"The people here were dying of hunger, for the sea was bringing them nothing but tragedy. So they resorted to their black slaves. They all did that, the poor and the great. They began selling them off at the cheapest prices. Dahma's mother heard that her owner was going to sell her, so she shut herself up in her tent and stayed for a whole day seized with fear and anxiety until she went mad."

"Why does my grandfather hate Dahma?"

My mother did not answer. Perhaps Dahma would forever be silent about her mother. Perhaps she was deterred—but by what? I resented my grandfather. I could sleep only for short periods and would sit up the whole night facing a wall that would split open and reveal the face of the woman soiled with silence and an uneasy smile.

Once at dawn Dahma put my head close to her face and there stole upon me a smell similar to that of earth upon which dawn's dew has fallen. "Don't annoy your poor mother," she said to me. "Your grandfather is not kindly."

Then, in the morning, I was standing by my grandfather's head. His features were exactly those of a pearling ship's captain who is practicing his calling by riding into the bodies of pearl-divers, inflating his ego by slaughtering them. But why should the woman be silent, while my grandfather openly flaunts his hatred of her? If he but knew that I cannot bear to be away from her he would strip my body of its heat.

I enjoy being with the woman. She makes me overflow with spiritual ideas that come to those who arrive by the path of the Prophet's Night Journey, while my grandfather wilts with the days at the woman's presence in our quarter.

One night of full moon, the mad poet rapped at my window with his stick and took me out with him to the woman's house. And what a stupendous sight I witnessed: the woman was at the peak of her beauty and vigor, her face filled with a mixture of sternness, a sense of peace, and deep pain. Her eyes had a purity about them that outshone the brilliance of a star or a desert under the umbrella of night. She had lit a fire in the middle of her house and was tirelessly feeding it with pieces of wood. Ouff! What an awesome movement she made as she approached the fire, more like that of a dancer combining joy and sadness, with words and meanings that were halfway between silence and speech.

The poet took me to a distant place. Under the full moon my whole being was replete with an all-encompassing sensation, for Dahma's beauty was oppressing me, was charging me with a burdensome joy and rapturous vision.

"Who is the woman? Why does my grandfather hate her? Is she a whore?"

The poet stroked away my apprehension. "The woman's mother went mad and the village killed her because she went about naked. Dahma stayed on with her master. She was an adolescent girl, and her beauty—as you can see—slays the lecher before the upright. Under cover of darkness he went to her bed, fortified by the fact that he was her legal owner. On the very first night he opened wide her legs and tied them to the foot of the bed. He continued to do so for several nights, bellowing with savage lust. His wife realized what was going on when the girl's stomach began to swell. She became filled with loathing for Dahma. She ordered the girl to hurl herself off some high place to bring about a miscarriage, and herself struck her on the neck and stomach, but the fetus remained in place. Then she put her out of the door."

I looked at Dahma. She was still gracefully bending and standing straight as she fed the fire. I saw there was a drum in her hand.

"She stayed alone in a hut of reeds. I brought her food, and after a while she gave birth to her child. Dahma was happy, delighted, dancing with joy. She sang plaintively when suckling the child. One day she stopped me from bringing her food, and she went out to look for work.

"And when one day she came back from work, she found her child had been butchered."

She began to rap lightly on the drum. Soon the sound grew louder, as the fire leapt up like red birds vanishing into space.

"After what happened to her son, I took her in. She was no longer talking and would maintain an awesome silence. Then one morning, she moved her tent right into where people lived in the middle of the village. I only appreciated the significance of this when the men of the village lost control of themselves and roamed around her hut like flies around honey."

Dahma's face was full of the rays of the moon and the night's shadows. She had clasped the drum to the hollow between her breasts as she rapped on it, with her head raised high like an animal when its jugular vein is to be severed.

"The rich went frantic, giving full rein to their base instincts."

"And did she have ten bast—?"

"She would choose the men. If one of them rushed off to her, she would remain with him for several days until she felt that her belly was with child. She would then lock herself up in her tent and keep aloof from men, while the man himself would continue to roam like a dog around the tent.

"And when she gave birth to her child, the reverberating echoes of a penetrating singing were heard in the village; they were heard in the houses and the alleyways and would seep through to the heart of every individual in the village. The sound of singing would continue until the woman had weaned her child, when she would carry him to his father's house. Since the child bore his very features, the father would attempt to conceal those of his own face. The complexion of the child was Dahma's, and the man's will was limp like a wet rag."

The woman began to sing, her voice growing louder, like the voice of a woman in labor.

"She did that with ten men . . . ."

"Then she has ten sons."

"She has dozens of songs that she sings. She does not stop singing, while the village screams. One of the men spoke truthfully about what happened to him with Dahma. He was crying like a child. Dahma, standing like a tree embraced by a desolate night, would cast herself down before him."

"Why does my grandfather hate her?"

"Your grandfather was one of them."

The woman stood upright and sang, and the madman sang with her. I went up close to Dahma. I felt dizzy, with something forming inside me like a ball and striking out in every direction. I clung to the woman and I sang. My grandfather, with his heart of a sea captain, struck out at me as he yelled, "She's insane. I'll flog her until the foreign spirit comes out from inside her. She's insane."

Threads of Delusion

Sheikha al-Nakhi

I was weaving in my imagination sweet longings and a beautiful image of my future life, an image that became bigger with the passing of the days and my intellectual and bodily growth. I was a small child when I would hear my mother telling me, whenever she had the opportunity and with the whole family present, that I was Ali's fiancée. Yes, his fiancée. "Would he find anyone better than her?" she would pronounce, "And she's as beautiful as the full moon." Then I grew up and my dreams and expectations grew bigger, as did my love for my cousin Ali, who filled my thoughts. I built dream castles and planned a wonderful picture of happiness, a happiness that would unite Ali and me in a single house, and we would have children who would fill our life with intimate joy. The day would come when the marriage rites would be performed and we would be the talk of the town. I would become lost in thought and would imagine the future as being very close and I would see myself as a bride clothed in a sparkling white wedding dress, my face aglow with happiness, surrounded by my girlfriends, sharing my joy with me. Then suddenly my thoughts came to a stop, as though I had been woken from a wonderful dream. I looked around me in bewilderment, asking: How had I allowed myself to toy with such thoughts?

Going to my room, I threw myself down on the bed and tried to gather my scattered thoughts, then reached out my hand and took up a book with which to kill that sense of boredom and weariness that had come over me. Right away, I heard my brother's voice, "Hossa, bring us some coffee."

I quickly prepared the coffee and was once again all attention. Arranging my bedraggled hair, I went to my brother's room. Pushing open the door, I walked with confused steps to the table in the middle of the room and put down the cups of coffee. Raising my head, I met the gaze of Ali, who had been engrossed in writing something and had then raised his head suddenly to say to me, "How are you, Hossa?" I couldn't reply. At that moment I had felt that my heart was a seagull hovering in the realm of happiness. I left the room quickly, sensing the blood almost bursting from my veins, hurried to my room, and closed the door. I seated myself on the edge of the bed and gave myself up to the dreams that wove beautiful pictures all around me, while all kinds of thoughts swarmed in my mind. Days were passing all too quickly and Ali would soon be going abroad for his studies. No, I couldn't imagine that. Ali, would you go without uttering a single word? Was your tongue incapable of speaking out? Or were you too shy? I just didn't know. Your silence tortures me.

◆

She awoke to the sound of the front door being closed. She looked out to make sure that Ali had left. Curiosity compelled her to go to her brother to find out what they had been talking about, hoping that she might hear some comforting words about her marriage to Ali.

She entered his room and sat down beside him, an engaging smile etched on her face. He raised his head, seeing in her looks various questions.

"What is it?"

"Nothing."

He wasn't satisfied with her answer, though he understood the significance of that single word.

"Ali came to say goodbye to me because, God willing, he's traveling tomorrow."

"Traveling? Tomorrow? Tomorrow, Ahmed?"

He nodded, at which she got up from where she had been sitting, a sense of bewilderment dragging her outside.

"He'll be traveling? And what about me? What about our future?"

A feeling of confusion took hold of her thoughts: If he was satisfied with me, he would have said something, wouldn't he?

"He travels and doesn't bother to give me so much as a farewell glance? Have I been living dreams woven by my own imagination?"

She tried to forget but was unable to, for Ali had long occupied her heart. The sweet days that had gone by still held beautiful images.

And now comes the letter that will do away with all her fears and doubts.

◆

"Open the door, Hossa."

It was her brother.

"Read this letter—it's from Ali."

From Ali at long last.

She reached out her hand, feeling joy mingled with fear and anxiety. It appeared to be addressed to her brother, but it would no doubt contain something relating to her. She thought, "Yes, I must read it."

Brother Ahmed,

Give me your blessing, for I have taken the step that is regarded as being half of one's religious duties—I have got married.

Too Late

Saleh Karama

His face showed signs of aging. He ran his hands over his feeble body, then felt the wrinkles on his face as he stood before the polished mirror, his face reflected in it like gold dust on the surface of water. Memories swirled in his mind. Our friend, 'Jumaa the garbage man,' moved away from the mirror and rubbed the rumpled hair on his head. He cursed the hour he had begun to work as a garbage man in the working class district, saying deep within himself, "I am Jumaa, even the children of the district stammer out my name wherever that unpleasant smell is diffused throughout the quarters of the district." A slight smile was traced on his face, then he added, "Such a very important man am I in the quarter's society that everyone calls out 'Jumaa thse garbage man is coming . . . Jumaa's arrived.'" These ideas took hold inside him and the sense of his continued and limitless importance rooted itself deep within his consciousness. Suddenly he burst out in a loud voice, "I am Jumaa the garbage man, an important man in the district. I am the top man." His screams echoed through the dilapidated room, dwindling away until they disappeared. He made up his mind to go out in order to carry out his usual work: the disposal of refuse scattered about under the houses and public utilities. His blue uniform disappeared behind the door of the closed building. On coming out of the door he found himself facing Hameed al-Khabeel, the madman of the quarter, the one who spread everyone's secrets and bits of news, for there was nothing he didn't know. Round and ball-shaped, he had a droll look about him and most of the people in the quarter would call him "the crazy one," though he wasn't crazy at all. Some people said that he was pretending to be mad, while others said that he had gone mad all of a sudden.

He approached Jumaa and shook him by the hand, a friendly smile lined on one side of his face, while his black intentions showed on the other. After that they indulged in some of the agreeable joking they enjoyed so as to clear away the early morning breezes replete with cold humidity. Said Jumaa the garbage man, "What about me, O crazy one? Am I not a very important man?"

The crazy one answered him, "Yes, you're important. Were it not for you the repulsive smells would have inundated everywhere and we'd no longer exist."

Jumaa took a deep breath and put on a proud look. Then he addressed himself, "I really am that important man." The queerest of ideas flashed into his mind as it came to him that tomorrow was the first of April, while today was the last day of March. He was further reminded of the fact because today he would be going to get his monthly pay packet, having completed his usual daily stint. The genius in him was transformed into something resembling invention, and his eyes bulged: it was as though he were searching for something that had been lost. While Hameed al-Khabeel had noticed these expressions, he had paid them no heed, except when, on the following day, Jumaa had uttered an April fool suggestion: "Why don't we make up a lie and have it ringing out all round the quarter and all the people of the quarter will weep and wail?" He was sunk in his thoughts when a new surprise sprang to mind and he called out at the top of his voice as though he'd discovered something funny. But at the same time he said, "Why don't you tell people that I've died suddenly at home. Such news will obviously shake the people of the quarter and they'll flock to my house to extend their condolences, especially when I'm a man on my own without a wife or children." Hameed al-Khabeel laughed, then said, "Do you want me to spread the news as of now?" Jumaa closed his eyes and stood pinned to the ground, looking toward the door of his house. He said, "Regard me right now as good as dead. Spread this precious news abroad for I am an important man— the garbage man. I have died alone at home."

He wandered round his home with its closed windows and broken doors, and he could perceive his vast sorrows in every corner. With the dawning of each radiant day those sorrows were shattered and transformed at night into a sound of roaring in an isolated place.

On a day that was overcast Jumaa stayed confined to his home, looking out through the door keyhole at the passersby. Three days went by without anyone from the quarter coming to offer their condolences except for his friend Hameed al-Khabeel, who spread far and wide with lightning speed the news of his death, roaming round the highways and byways saying that Jumaa the garbage man had died. The news made no impression on the quarter and no attention was paid to his death. Jumaa himself continued, with the eyes of a hawk, to stare out at the passersby as though imploring them to come to him.

This time the night weighed heavily upon him. His feelings began to be encircled by the cold and he was visited by extraordinary dreams as though he were crossing space, swimming in hot waters, and writhing on burning coals.

A week passed and no one came to knock at his home, not a single human being came anywhere near his door. The anxieties that come with solitude began to reign over every corner of the house and his old broken-down room. The smell of the lie was everywhere, and in the deluge of his reverberating collapse hot tears flowed down his cheeks, ending up in his scraggy beard. No one had imagined this terrible ending.

No one had imagined that one day he would lie to himself with such ease and come to believe himself to be an important person.

A garbage person who the people of the quarter could not manage without. The horrible smell submerged the whole quarter and would increase whenever the cold winter winds blew and produced runny noses. People kept away from the neighboring districts and from visiting this quarter itself, because of its many gnats and heaps of rubbish. There were signs of a belated recognition that a search should be made for a man the quarter had lost and was in need of. People gathered in front of the mosque in lines, with muffled noses, looking distracted. The question that was on everyone's lips was, "Where is Jumaa the garbage man?" Some of them said, "We've heard he's died—according to Hameed al-Khabeel." The crowds moved off in the direction of Jumaa's house, led by Sheikh Saad in a grave procession to look into the matter of his disappearance. On arriving at his house, they found the door open. When they entered they were brought to a halt by the sound of loud wailing coming from the dilapidated room. When they burst into it they found a shrouded body and Hameed al-Khabeel next to it weeping and sobbing. When al-Khabeel saw them, he raised his head and shouted at them, "Now you have found out his real worth after he has committed suicide because he himself has discovered the real truth—he found out that man has no value in life, and especially in your community."

Two Neighbors | *Muhammad al-Murr*

Having placed him in his bed and covered him up, the nurse went to her chair at the end of the large room. Turning to his right, he found that the bed was unoccupied, then he turned to his left and found that he had a neighbor.

"Good evening," he said to his neighbor.

"Good evening to you. Why didn't you scream when the nurse brought you?"

"Why should I scream? I'm not suffering from anything."

"But most of those who are brought here arrive with prolonged screams."

"Perhaps the reason for such screaming was either pain or surprise. My own birth was quite normal and natural."

"What's your name?"

"I don't know. They haven't yet chosen a name for me—I'm only four hours old."

"My parents chose a name for me during the first month of pregnancy. I was the first child. When the doctor told my father that my mother was pregnant, he almost kissed her."

"The doctor or your mother?"

"The doctor, of course. My mother had had enough of being kissed. So, when the news of her pregnancy came three months after they were married, as we were returning home in the car, my father chose two names: Butti and Hamda, making allowances for either possibility. They were of course the name of his grandfather and the name of his late mother. My mother agreed to the name Hamda, saying that it was a beautiful name, being derived from the root letters meaning 'praise'—my mother's a teacher of Arabic—but she rejected the name Butti, as it was a negative name and she didn't want her son to be called by a name derived from a root that indicated sluggishness. She would like a name that suggested liveliness and dynamism, or a name that indicated eminence and nobility, or had hints of poetical sweetness. The discussion continued at home for the whole day, and by evening my mother had won the battle and had wheedled my father into agreeing to the name she liked."

"And what was that?"

"Said—a nice name, don't you think?"

"Yes, I believe so."

"It is, incidentally, her father's name, my grandfather. As for you, didn't they choose a name for you while you were still inside?"

"No, I came by mistake."

"How's that?"

"They've got five children: three boys and two girls. My mother believed that this was the ideal number for a happy family, while my father wanted a smaller family, and he was always saying, 'The mother hawk gives birth to only a few. I wanted a few brave hawks, not a whole lot of scared rabbits.' After the fifth child my mother began using contraceptive pills with diligent care, but sometimes taking precautions doesn't work against fate and she was confronted unexpectedly by the symptoms of pregnancy which were confirmed by the doctor."

"What did your father do?"

"He flew into a rage, and the months of pregnancy, especially the first few, were filled with accusations and squabbles, with my father accusing my mother of negligence and carelessness in using the pills, hinting that she'd done it on purpose to wear him out with children so that he wouldn't take a second wife, and that she herself wanted to have many children so that they would vie with one another in caring for her in her old age."

"And what was your mother's reaction?"

"My mother's a cheerful soul and she'd respond to each accusation with a joke, and to each cry of anger with a smile. My brothers and sisters would play about rowdily. The oldest boy, who was attached to his father, would say, 'We'll strangle him in the cradle,' while the middle boy said, 'We'll throw him in the sea,' with the youngest saying, 'We'll poison him.' The two girls were in sympathy with me, and the youngest said, 'The one on the way will be a girl and so we'll be three girls against three boys.' The eldest girl said, 'She'll go with us to the markets and the beauty salons.' I don't think they'll be happy now that the two of them know that the new arrival was a boy. How old are you?"

"Four days. We were supposed to go home yesterday but the doctor said that I had a slight bit of jaundice and I was in need of some care."

"Nothing to worry about, you need some water and sugar and a little exposure to the sun and you'll quickly recover."

"How do you know that?"

"From my mother. When I was in the third month, she went to visit her sister whose little newborn girl was ill with jaundice, which frightened my aunt, but my mother reassured her. Have they circumcised you?"

"Yes, on the second day."

"Did you find the operation painful?"

"Yes, a bit."

"Did you cry?"

"No."

"Why not?"

"The doctor was laughing, so I laughed with him. When they brought me to my mother after the operation and told her about it, she laughed and so did I. Then, when my father came to visit us and they told him about the operation, he laughed and my mother laughed and I laughed with them. And when my grandmother and my aunts visited us and they heard what had happened, they all laughed and I laughed with them."

"You'll laugh a lot in your life."

"Why?"

"Because you're the first boy and perhaps you'll be the only one. Who's to know?"

"You, too, you'll be laughing a lot."

"How's that?"

"You're the last of the litter and they'll smother you with pampering and choke you with their hugs and kisses."

"What I heard during the months of pregnancy suggested that they'd be choking me but not with kisses."

"Put aside these depressing thoughts, haven't you noticed that people say things and then do the opposite?"

"Yes, sometimes, but at other times they say things and carry them out to the letter."

"Life has two sides, negative and positive. Expect the best."

"And if the worst occurs?"

"Don't be pessimistic."

"I'm not pessimistic, but what has happened to me makes me expect the worst."

"How's that?"

"In the first months of pregnancy, my grandmother used to visit us, and on hearing my father's angry, bitter words would say, 'You don't deserve this heaven-sent gift. I'll take him from you and bring him up and make him the apple of my eye.' A month ago she was hit by a car and is now in a wheelchair, in need of someone to look after her and make her the apple of his eye."

"Poor thing; at any rate don't be too upset, everything's going to be fine for both of you. My mother was extremely frightened about the birth, and when she talked to her doctor and her married women friends about the pains of childbirth, most of them were indescribably severe and unpleasant. One of them said, 'It's a small death,' while her neighbor said, 'You'll curse the day you married,' while another neighbor added, 'In fact you'll curse the very day you were born.' One night my mother saw a television film late at night that showed the heroine giving birth with cries of pain and she was overcome with panic. My father was away, and she didn't sleep the whole night despite her evident tiredness, having attended her cousin's wedding party."

"She went to a wedding party when she was pregnant?"

"Yes, she was in the ninth month. During the period of her pregnancy she attended ten wedding parties."

"Didn't she get tired or embarrassed at her appearance with her protruding stomach?"

"Not at all, in fact she used to go to those parties all dressed up."

"How extraordinary, when my mother gets pregnant she cuts herself off from all social engagements and wears only her oldest clothes and has nothing to do with kohl for her eyes and all cosmetics."

"Two different attitudes. Coming back to my mother on that night, the screaming birth scene caused her such terror that she stayed awake in bed, with me awake alongside her until daybreak, after which we slept for a couple of welcome hours. When I came out into the world, she did not scream or bite her fingers or tear the pillow with her teeth; it seems that the pain she had had been like the nibbling of a young wolf when she had expected to be torn to pieces by a savage lion. And so she doesn't get frightened and doesn't expect catastrophes to occur. You and your grandmother will be just fine."

"I don't know. While she was giving birth my mother let out some terrible screams and her whole face and body went into contractions, and she grasped hold of the hands of the doctor and the nurses so hard that she hurt them, leaving marks on their arms. She was jabbering words expressing pain, fear, anger, and rage."

"Your birth was a difficult one?"

"No, it was a normal one according to the doctor, but it seems that my mother had got used to behaving this way from previous childbirths."

"Did your father give the call to prayer in your ear?"

"No, my father didn't attend the birth. He went off to spend the weekend at his partner's farm. And you?"

"My father gave the call to prayer in my ear twice. On the first occasion he was so overcome with joy that he made a mistake and had to do it again."

"Didn't I tell you that you'll be lucky and pampered?"

"Too much pampering is bad for one. My uncle was the only boy and the pampering he got led him to become a heroin addict and he's now an inmate of a sanatorium. Also, you can have bad luck."

"How do you mean?"

"I may get diabetes when I'm a child so that my body is pierced with insulin injections and I spend the rest of my life sickly and taking precautions, meaning I can't lead a normal life like other people. Or perhaps I am stricken with a fear of people so that I live a life of isolation surrounded by walls of doubt and suspicion, or maybe I am mentally retarded so that I'm prevented from studying, becoming simple-minded, an object of ridicule to others and of pity to my family."

"No, none of these things will happen to you. You just say that so as to keep away the evil eye."

"And what's this evil eye?"

"The eye of envy. My mother does that all the time. While our financial position is good, my mother complains all the time of being poor. My brother and sisters are as fit as horses, while she says that they are continuously ill. She complains a lot to people about her heart though the doctor has told her that her heart is like that of a young girl."

"But there's such a thing as bad luck. You told me about what happened to your grandmother. Listen, then, to what happened to mine, my father's mother. She had a millionaire brother who had no sons. He was ten years older than her and he had some half a dozen things wrong with him. In the event of his death she was going to inherit half his fortune, around a hundred million dirhams, while the rest would go to his wife and his half-brother. She went to Munich with her two daughters where she had check-ups that confirmed that she was in excellent health. On going out with her daughters and grandchildren for a walk near the royal palace, she stayed on a while to look in a shop window when she was trampled down by one of those big horses that pull the tourist cabs. She perished beneath the horse's hooves and thus my father and his brothers and sisters lost their mother and a hundred million dirhams which would now go to the rest of the inheritors."

"You call it bad luck, but my mother calls it the evil eye. What did your grandfather do to have all that wealth?"

"He inherited the money and properties of his father."

"And what did his father work at?"

"He was a vicious money lender who loved planting date palms of various kinds. People used to laugh at him when he put up fences around the vast sandy tracks in which he had planted some date palms. Land had no value in those days—it was buildings that were worth something, and even they were moderately priced. They thought he was a bit crazy—the curse of being a money lender."

"And what did your grandfather do?"

"He didn't do anything."

"How's that?"

"He was extremely lazy. He was addicted to playing dominoes in the café and adored going to sleep, and would sometimes sleep for two days running. He was right—sleep's wonderful, isn't it?"

"Yes, indeed. And what happened after that?"

"After spending thirty years sleeping and playing dominoes my grandfather woke up and found that the value of the properties he'd inherited from his father had increased five hundred times, and sometimes by a thousand and two thousand times, and had proved that the opposite of the popular saying was true, that good luck lay not in being active, but in laziness and sleep. During her pregnancy my mother used to say that I was worth more than a hundred million!"

"Did she mean she was repaying your father by producing you?"

"No, she wanted to let everyone know how much she loved me. She's an emotional and sensitive woman sometimes. When she is affected by certain sad songs she cries, and when she listens to joyful songs with lively tunes she dances."

"Even during pregnancy?"

"Yes, in the first months of course. Most of these times would be when she was alone in front of the big mirror in the bedroom, and on a few other occasions when she'd be with her very close women friends."

"My mother doesn't dance, and even if she were to try, it would be difficult for her as her weight never drops below ninety kilos.

She just adores sweets—they are her greatest passion in life. Despite her love for joking and jollity, she cries a lot; she cries when watching sad scenes in sentimental films, she cries when her children fall ill, she cries when she remembers her late sister, and she cries when she snips her finger when cutting the meat."

"She cries easily?"

"Yes, and her perpetual nightmare is the possibility that my father might take a second wife."

"Would he do so?"

"Who? My father? God forbid! He believes that his marriage to my mother was the greatest mistake of his life!"

"He doesn't like women?"

"He flees from them as a healthy man flees from the plague."

"Why?"

"He doesn't understand them. He wasn't at ease with his mother, he wasn't at ease with his wife, and he wasn't at ease with his daughter. If women were to disappear off the surface of the earth he wouldn't be affected. His one and only hobby has nothing to do with women."

"And what is that hobby?"

"Breeding pigeons. He spends long happy hours before nightfall examining the pigeons' cages on the roof of our house and feeding them and setting off the breeds which fly by the famous 'heart method,' and when my mother comes to ask him if there is anything he wants of her, he replies with utter indifference, 'To separate from you.'"

"Isn't she upset by this answer?"

"Slightly. She knows that she intrudes on his delightful moments spent in the paradise of his pigeons."

"Hasn't she tried to join him in this hobby of his?"

"She can't—she's got a sensitivity to pigeons."

"Sensitivity! How can that be? Pigeons are nice clean birds."

"Touching pigeons brings my mother out in red spots on her arms and legs. Sometimes she scratches them so much that they bleed."

"How terribly strange!"

"After which she has to have a long treatment with tablets and injections."

"They gave me an injection on the second day. They said it was an inoculation against pneumonia. I don't know what sort of illness that is."

"It's an illness that makes you cough until you die."

"How do you know that?"

"From my mother. Talking about the various sorts of illnesses is one of her favorite hobbies and she's never bored talking about them, especially when it's a disease suffered by her friends and relatives. Did the injection hurt?"

"Yes, didn't they give you an injection?"

"No, perhaps tomorrow. What's this business of childbirth? From the beginning one has painful injections."

"And your mother has a sensitivity."

"And you've got jaundice."

"You got it through infantile paralysis."

"And you lost a million dirhams."

"Don't give such matters too much thought."

"How can't I—it's the beginning, only the beginning."

The nurse came in carrying a newborn whose screams shook the night's peace.

"Good heavens!—and all this screaming too."

"Don't worry. Good night."

The newcomer's screaming intensified. The two neighbors closed their eyes, though one of them continued his thoughts.

Zaain and Fatima | *Mohamed al-Mazrouei*

Had he known that the operation for varicose veins he had done on his legs would be a sign that things were going to improve for him, and that with it he'd be marrying, he'd have had it done ages ago.

Those were his thoughts when, at the age of sixty, he had held the pen to sign his marriage contract. The whole thing had been a matter of more than thirty-one years, much of which he had spent standing in front of her house, recollecting all the tales of the lovers of old that the inhabitants of the Powerhouse Quarter used to recount so that he had become something of an object of fun.

"Man, the oil came out from under your feet"—meaning that he'd been standing around for far too long. It was a saying his brother would use with him whenever he saw him standing in front of the door of the house. Their two houses were opposite one another, and she was always to be found behind the window facing him. Thirty-one years filled with incidents and lives that had meant nothing to the two of them because all they were waiting for was to be brought together under the same roof.

In his twenties, and in the 1970s, and after the announcement that the Trucial States had become one federal state, he had gone on his own to her father in his shop and had asked for her hand in marriage.

"You're a man," the father said to him, "and you know the ways of the Arabs. How do you ask for a girl in marriage and your own family don't know about it?"

What he said wasn't devoid of reason and he had many different reasons for refusing, and all Zaain's attempts at persuading his family that she should become engaged to him failed. They were always repeating, "If a date palm were to sprout out from your head, we wouldn't let you get engaged to this non-Arab girl."

He spent the beginning of his life in sorrow at this state of affairs, while she was adamant in not accepting anyone else; it was either him or no one. She was deprived of completing her education and had become a prisoner between the walls of her house because of the doubts that had made their way to her father's heart.

As for him, his appetite had deserted him at the beginning and he grew thin because of the small amount of food he consumed. In fact he quite calmly reached the stage where he felt no need to put anything in his stomach. People would try to give him hope saying that by eating he'd become engaged to her, but after he'd eaten they'd say to him, "Knock your head against the wall—the food you've eaten will keep you going for a week."

And like every person in love this would keep on recurring without his learning any lesson from it, that perhaps they were telling the truth once and that it would happen. It didn't mean that he wanted to die by suicide, just that the sickness of love and separation had taken its toll of him. In no way did he want to be separated from his loved one, even by death.

He found all sorts of arguments for standing in front of the window of her house, which was when the varicose veins began to ruin his legs, leaving protruding blue veins that formed a map of love of a different kind. Zaain was in his mid-forties when the place changed, villas replacing the local-style houses that had been witnesses to his story. His footprints, which had long made their impression on the street sands, were no longer to be seen on the asphalt, for the state had begun to develop the old quarters and to devise new planning for the area. His house and several other houses became part of a plan to extend the main street. The owners received compensation in the form of money and an alternative site in a distant district, as had happened in other cases. Yet even so he would spend the greater part of his day close to her blurred shape behind the window.

The doctor who carried out his operation and knew about his story told him, after he had woken up from the anesthetic, "Now you can begin your story anew, for your legs are much better now."

But he had made plans to travel outside the Emirates, and after he had spent two years abroad, he had news of his father's death. His family had busied themselves with their own lives, each brother and sister with their spouses and children who had themselves grown up and become fathers. With the change in social climate and way of life, no one cared any longer, as they used to do, about either him or her. Family clannishness no longer presented the kind of obstacles it had in the past. Thus had life changed after more than thirty years.

With an intimation from her, and with the remaining years he had, he went into the shop of her father, now the owner of a jeweler's which was run by her brother, to find that her family too had become more flexible, and there was no one there in their old house apart from an old woman who kept Fatima company. Her brothers were also busy with their families and this stranger no longer presented a problem for them, so they had agreed to his marrying her. It was the best solution to her not remaining a spinster who lived in their father's house, which could bring them in millions of dirhams.

The marriage contract was fixed and, like any common stranger, his family had accepted the invitation, overlooking their part in having delayed the marriage for more than three decades.

"Fine, fine, this poor girl has waited far too long."

Thus spoke those who were concerned with it.

In the meantime neither Fatima nor Zaain worried about anything except being together, for they did not wish to lose any more time.

The Story of Ibrahim

Roda al-Baluchi

His two small eyes glistened under the tears, and the trembling of his great body was like that of a dilapidated building on the verge of collapse. It was with difficulty that he was able to stand, the trunk of the date palm acting as a convenient prop for his hand. Then he shuffled along on feet weighed down with chains shackled round them, and didn't turn to me. Before he got too far away I called out to him from behind, "Ibrahim, don't be annoyed. I was just joking. Come along so that we finish our game."

He didn't answer me but continued with his funny way of walking, then tried to run with his bare feet, which time had transformed into a pair of shoes of dark brown scaly leather.

No one had previously seen this young man, who was approaching the age of twenty, not wearing these fetters. The people in our village were positive that it was his mother, Alaash, who had fastened the chains around his feet, fearing that he might escape from her as his father had done before him. She had then got rid of the key to the chains by throwing it down the hole of the lavatory in her old house—or so the women of our village claimed.

I caught up with him and implored him to return so that we could finish the game, but he didn't reply. He stumbled against a medium-sized stone deeply embedded in the earth, fell heavily to the ground, and burst into loud, anguished crying that would not stop. Like a small child he let out violent sobs until I took pity on him. He quietened down a little and stopped weeping, though remaining silent, neither answering me nor raising his head. I tried to calm him by patting him on his frizzed hair and kissing him on his forehead, which smelled of sweat.

"I love you, Ibrahim," I whispered in his ear. "By God the Almighty I love you, even without any sweets."

His breathing slowed down. It rose like a sand dune, then plummeted, while he did not reply to my smile. His eyes were fixed on the wet earth and his rough hand played with the powdery sand. His voice issued diffidently from his chest.

"And I too," he assured me, "love you by God the Almighty."

Then it wasn't long before he gave a laugh.

Plunging headlong into his chest, guffawing with laughter, I placed my hand in his dark-skinned one to help him to his feet. We then returned together to the ravine of date palms to complete the game we had started there. Ibrahim was laughing, his dirty teeth showing, all flushed with excitement and forgetting that only minutes ago I had shouted at him and threatened never to play with him again, that our friendship would come to an end if he didn't find some way of bringing me some sweets as he did every day. He would take advantage of his mother and steal into one of the rooms she had converted to a shop for selling candies and ices to the village children. She also sold things required by women, such as pieces of cloth, gallabiyas, veils and head-coverings, combs, certain types of perfumes, and cheap sorts of makeup that she would generally bring from the markets of Dubai when she ran out of them. It seemed, though, that Ibrahim's mother had found out about his small acts of thievery;

having scolded him sharply, she had locked the door of her shop with a key to which she had attached a piece of string so that she could hang it around her neck.

One day I asked my mother about Ibrahim's father: why didn't he come to see his son?

She had answered, "He traveled to another town and settled down there, having married a divorced woman who was barren and older than him. He had fallen in love with her after he had met her on one of his travels to the town. Two years later he had separated from Ibrahim's mother, the wife who had given him a son. There was no longer any news of him in the village and his only son also knew nothing of him. Ibrahim's mother had refused all who had sought her hand in marriage, having taken the decision to devote herself to her son whom she loved dearly because of his great likeness to his father, both having the same deep way of looking when they laughed, though as he got older the son showed increasing signs of being mentally disturbed."

We played together, he and I, without our being conscious of the passage of time, then, all at once, I remembered that I had to return home before my mother became aware of my prolonged absence and punished me by locking me up for a whole day. Ibrahim asked that we go back together and that I accompany him to the built-up area, as he was frightened to go on his own. I contemplated the shackles on his feet, thinking that if I were to accompany him I'd be late getting back. I raised my head and looked toward his lofty frame, which separated us by a whole twelve years. I uttered my question with irritated impatience, "When are you going to get rid of these rusty shackles of yours?"

He answered me in a perplexed tone, "I don't know. My mother says that these chains protect me from getting lost, and that I mustn't allow anyone to remove them from my feet, otherwise I'll get lost and won't know the way back home."

I was not convinced by his reply and continued to stare into his brown gaunt face before answering him jokingly.

"Hey, grown-ups don't get lost, and you're grown up, Ibrahim. You're even older than I am and older than Khalifa, Saoud, and Mubarak, so how can you get lost?"

My answer baffled him, so he kept silent. I paid him no mind and went off, ignoring his pleas imploring me to stop. His ranting shouts only spurred me on to quicken my steps without turning back so that his voice died away little by little.

The following morning I caught cold and took to my bed for a whole week and was forced to drink the burning herbal concoction that my grandmother prepared from ginger and honey. I knew for sure that Ibrahim was waiting for me to come out to him from early morning, waiting on the small hillock that was only a few meters away from our house. For my sake he wouldn't heed the afflictions of the scorching sun as it burnt his emaciated face and brought on feelings of thirst, while his eyes were glued to the front door. He would lower his head when he spotted my father as he left for work and wouldn't have the courage to knock at the door for fear that my grandmother might come out and threaten to skin him alive with a beating. Quarrelsome boys would harass him whenever they spotted him there and would throw anything that lay to hand at him. They would also hurl abuse at him, jeering at him with mocking phrases they had learned from Ibrahim's companions when they had been his age and who had subsequently grown up without him following suit.

He would stand where he was without moving, incapable of resisting their hurtful mocking, merely hoping that I would come out to him at any moment to defend him as usual. But none of that would happen this time. My real concern was for one single thing, namely that Ibrahim shouldn't believe that I was perhaps making my escape from him after the supply of sweets he used to bring me had come to a stop. I was frightened that he would think badly of me, and I prayed to God that no one might harm him so that he might be cured of his ailment.

The morning came when I felt that the state of my health had greatly improved and I was in a hurry to meet my friends, including Ibrahim. I went out to play with some of my companions at the nearby hill after they had invited me to join them for a game of football, an invitation I had accepted with great enthusiasm. We were engrossed in the game when one of them shouted out, "Look over there—the madman's running."

He was pointing at Ibrahim who, surprisingly, was completely free of his shackles. He was running and guffawing at the top of his voice, using his feet like a bird that has been set free. His mother was running after him, in a state of bewilderment, her hair disheveled. She was calling out to him and imploring him to return, but he just went on running like a mountain partridge. Having caught sight of us there, she asked us to bring him back to her, promising us that she'd reward us all with sweets and ice cream if we succeeded in catching him. This spurred us on to run even faster after him, but he slipped through our hands like a piece of soap, running with such speed that we couldn't believe our eyes that Ibrahim, who had spent the greater part of his life walking around like a sick tortoise, could now run at such a crazy speed.

It became clear that the distance between us was increasing, as more people, young and old, joined in the chase. Everyone was rushing along, with Ibrahim out in front, until we had gone beyond the outskirts of the village, all of us panting with exhaustion and with Ibrahim laughing at the top of his voice. All were amazed at this extraordinary sight, and all too soon it became difficult to make out Ibrahim's features as he drew away and then disappeared from sight.

About the Authors

Abdul Hamid Ahmed was born in 1957 in Dubai. He received a degree in psychology and began writing short stories in the early 1970s. He has published three volumes of short stories and several collections of essays. He is editor in chief of the English-language newspaper *Gulf News*.

Roda al-Baluchi was born in 1975 in al-Ain. Her first collection of short stories was published in Abu Dhabi in 2008.

Hareb al-Dhaheri, born in al-Ain in 1964, studied computer science and business administration in the United States. He has published two volumes of short stories, of which two stories were previously published in English. He works for the oil company ADNOC and is the director of the Union of Emirati Writers.

Nasser al-Dhaheri, born in al-Ain in 1960, received a degree in journalism and French literature from UAE University and continued his studies at the Sorbonne. He has worked in journalism and was editor of *al-Ittihad* newspaper. He used to write a monthly travel column and has published nine volumes of articles and short stories. His short stories have been translated into English, French, and Russian.

Maryam Jumaa Faraj was born in the Emirates. She received a degree from UAE University in 1980 and is studying for a doctorate in translation. She has published two volumes of short stories.

Nasser Jubran is the consultant to the cultural department of the state of Ajman.

Saleh Karama is a retired army officer who has published one volume of short stories.

Jumaa al-Fairuz was born in Ras al-Khaimah and died in 2001. He graduated in 1975 with a degree in music from Cairo. He made over forty musical compositions and produced several collections of short stories. He also worked in the UAE ministry of information and culture.

Lamees Faris al-Marzuqi was born Abu Dhabi in 1977. She graduated from the University of Ajman in 1999 and has been a teacher since. She has published in newspapers and is about to publish her first novel.

Mohamed al-Mazrouei, born in Egypt in 1962, has published five volumes of poetry and one volume of short stories. He is also an abstract artist and has held several exhibitions in the Emirates.

Ebtisam al-Mualla is a member of the Emirates Writers Union and has published a number of short stories in local newspapers.

Ibrahim Mubarak was born in 1952 in Dubai and obtained a degree in psychology, and a diploma from the Teachers' College in Dubai. He is the director of cultural and artistic activities at the ministry of education and youth. He has published five volumes of short stories.

Muhammad al-Murr was born in Dubai and received his later education at Syracuse University in New York. He has published thirteen volumes of short stories and is the best-known writer in the Emirates. His stories have also been published in English translation.

Sheikha al-Nakhi, born in 1952 in Sharjah, received a degree from UAE University in 1985 and was one of the earliest short-story writers in the Emirates. She has published two volumes of short stories.

Maryam Al Saedi received a degree in English literature from UAE University. She is about to publish her first collection of short stories.

Omniyat Salem, born in the Emirates in 1971, has published one volume of short stories.

Salma Matar Seif, born in 1961 in Ajman, is a short-story writer. Her story in this collection originally appeared in *Under the Naked Sky: Short Stories from the Arab World* (AUC Press, 2000).

Ali Abdul Aziz al-Sharhan worked as minister of education and youth in the UAE. He holds a PhD in linguistics from the University of Essex and is a member of the Emirates Writers Union. He has published several collections of short stories.

Muhsin Soleiman was born in Sharjah in 1976 and works in Dubai International Airport. His work has been published in local newspapers, *al-Khaleej* and *al-Bayan*, and he has published one collection of short stories. His work has won awards in Sharjah and Alexandria.

'A'ishaa al-Za'aby was born in Ras al-Khaimah in 1972. She holds a degree in education and works as a teacher in Ajman. She has published two collections of short stories.